This would be her very last chance to be a different woman.

She would go to the ball wearing the dress Mr. Rushworth had sent her and she would enjoy it. For once. Without thinking of others or imagining consequences. The consequences of her life thus far were brutally real, and a small wonderment would not go amiss.

Mr. Rushworth was not ordinary or insignificant, but then neither would he stay with her for long, their pledge a temporary thing while he found his feet here in England and his place near the sea. After that she would have served her purpose, a shield and a ploy, and he would go back to the life he was born to. A would-be lord and a man next in line to the title of baron.

She would be thirty-one in two days, the years of her life running down into middle age. No, the chance of a fairy-tale night in a golden dress and pearls was too good an opportunity to miss simply because of fear. She would swallow up her misgivings and enjoy it. She was determined that she would.

SOPHIA JAMES

The Spinster's Scandalous Affair

HARLEQUIN

HISTORICAL

HARLEQUIN®
HISTORICAL™

Recycling programs
for this product may
not exist in your area.

ISBN-13: 978-1-335-50623-8

The Spinster's Scandalous Affair

Copyright © 2021 by Sophia James

This is a work of fiction. Names, characters, places and incidents
are either the product of the author's imagination or are used fictitiously.
Any resemblance to actual persons, living or dead, businesses,
companies, events or locales is entirely coincidental.

This edition published by arrangement with Harlequin Books S.A.

For questions and comments about the quality of this book,
please contact us at CustomerService@Harlequin.com.

Harlequin Enterprises ULC
22 Adelaide St. West, 40th Floor
Toronto, Ontario M5H 4E3, Canada
www.Harlequin.com

Printed in U.S.A.

Sophia James lives in Chelsea Bay, on the North Shore of Auckland, New Zealand, with her husband, who is an artist. She has a degree in English and history from Auckland University and believes her love of writing was formed by reading Georgette Heyer on vacations at her grandmother's house. Sophia enjoys getting feedback at Facebook.com/sophiajamesauthor.

Content Note

The Spinster's Scandalous Affair
features a sexual assault, which some
readers may find difficult.

Prologue

He came towards the bed, his gaze on hers, the night-time casting shadow across his eyes and sending long planes of angle to his cheeks.

Beautiful.

His beauty had always soothed her, made her relax into the moment, made it easier and simpler. Made it right.

She moved as his finger touched her lip, tracing the line in a gentle caress, feeling him there, understanding his presence, knowing that he only meant to keep her safe. He did not speak and she was glad of it as their fingers entwined, softly and without duress. She leant into him, skin on skin, close and sheathed against the chill.

He didn't kiss her—he never did—but his mouth brushed across the fragile skin on her neck.

She did not pull away. She did not open her eyes either to find the light. Rather, she ran her tongue across the warmth of him, tasting...salt and muskiness, the flavour of a man in moonlight.

Different from usual.

She stilled because this was another set of rules, a new game that was more dangerous than the one before, and if he smiled he hid it from her, mirth caught in the corners of his mouth, ever hungry for what came next...

The clock on the mantel chimed four loud, discordant noises which altered her truths. Her body tensed and memory returned, the chills of a nightmare taking over from the fluid realm of dreams.

'No?'

A question lingered within the meaning.

'No.' She repeated it again, but he was gone already, away from her dreams, like Aladdin in the bottle, eliminated to a netherworld far from this one.

Sweat beaded under her arms and in the creases of her breasts, like a warning as shaking fingers came to her lips to feel the flesh there. Shame. Even a wasteland held signposts and hers were here with force.

Don't. Don't. Don't.

'Please God, help me.'

The plea formed even as she meant it not to, a pitiful appeal to a deity who would have far better things to do. Help me what? Help me to forget? Help me to remember? Help me to understand that I am not as other woman are and never will be?

She reached for the blanket beside her and draped it across her shoulders before standing and walking to the window. It was cold outside, a flurry of rain blurring the light from a lamp tied to its place at the far end of the pathway. A winter city and no warmth in sight. She felt frost on the air even through the glass and shivered.

Her leg ached and she stretched, trying to relieve the pain. The cold made it worse, the bone in her lower leg having been badly mended and now letting her know it.

The sum of all her parts was lessening with each successive year, she thought then. Almost thirty-one and the hopes of something different fading with the passing months.

Her stepmother's snores vibrated through the thin wall between them, a constant cacophony of sound, the cough with which the older woman was afflicted worsening her constitution.

With care she traced her initials into the condensation on the glass and surrounded it by the shape of a heart. ED. The letters dripped away to a misshapen nothingness, much like she herself was doing, though this time the thought made her smile.

Her imagination had always got the better of her, always raced on to places that should not exist, but this night-time dream had been a recurrent one for years now, the face of shadowed beauty dear and trusted, a dream so far removed from reality that it felt safe.

She tried to bring him back in wakefulness—a lover who was circumspect and polite and who answered her bidding exactly—but she failed.

Tonight, however, her actions had been surprising. Usually there was a quiet embrace and a soft caress. This new sensuality was worrying for she could not understand the intent. Would it happen again? The church bells of Westminster pealed into the night, marking the next quarter.

Only those whose souls were bothered were up at this time, the dawn creeping closer, the world about to wake.

She wished she might return to her bed and sleep but knew that she couldn't, every fibre in her body thrumming with a feeling that was altered.

A barren and ageing spinster who'd had her chance and failed at it. She knew there wouldn't be another.

Chapter One

London—Tuesday, February 1st, 1814

Augustus Anthony Andrew Rushworth arrived back in London just in time to witness the long, hard frost of 1814. The wind blew his full-sailed schooner up the Thames with a cold and singular fury, past the rows of other vessels waiting to be docked, hulls deep in the water with unloaded cargo.

It was ten years since he had last been home and the city looked busier and bigger, the frozen river before Bankside in the distance sporting tents and stalls and revellers, banners and flags blowing in the wind.

'It's the Frost Fair, sir,' Mr Thomas Pemberton beside him noted. 'And a sight to behold, is it not?'

Augustus's glance passed over the display of people and tents on the ice. Everywhere there was movement, figures dark against the white, and smoke plumes rising from the lit fires. Blackfriars Bridge with its semi-elliptical arches stood to one side of all the movement and London Bridge was on the other, no water anywhere to be seen in between. The voices of vendors hung on the wind, a sing-song cadence working hard to attract the next sale.

The severe cold was part of the reason the ship had been late docking, the drifts of dangerous ice numerous, some even reaching as far as the sea. Further up from here the river was completely frozen over, he'd been told, and he could well believe it.

With the sails lowering and flapping, Augustus felt displaced, the dark cold of England different from the bright warmth of India. Fog swirled on the water, the rising damp in the air so noticeable that he pulled up his collar.

'It's been the coldest Christmas on record, sir, and London is a lot changed compared to what it was like when you left it, I suppose?' As if realising his mistake, Pemberton continued quickly. 'And now that your father is no longer with us…' His grandfather's factor tailed off, cheeks reddening.

Once, Augustus might have cared, but that emotion had long since gone and he'd returned to England for neither love nor reconciliation. He wondered why any of this could still hurt him, so long after the fact. So many years had passed, so many miles between who he had been and who he was now.

'The Rushworth town house in St James's is at your disposal, Mr Rushworth. I have had it readied at the behest of your grandfather.'

'Thank you.'

Swallowing, he tried to smile, hating the way his fingers shook against the wool of his coat. Even the simple gestures were hard sometimes, but Pemberton was talking again so he made himself listen.

'Your grandfather is expecting you at Amerleigh House. He asked me to relay his best wishes and bade me tell you that—'

The words were cut off as the deck beneath them shook and August's hands shot out to grip the nearby rail for balance. Ice against wood was a jarring hit, but it was also a welcome reprieve from words he had no desire to hear.

Already they were shouting, the sailors and the dockhands, the call of business drowning out conversation. Above them, gulls wheeled, looking for food, no doubt, though the tea, spices and cloth in the holds of the *Minerva* would have little sustenance to offer them. Ropes appeared from nowhere and were bound against ancient bollards lining the dock and securing anchorage. Further afield he could see numerous lads, who had been jumping off the small splintered ice cliffs a moment earlier, stop and stare at the bulky ship coming into port.

A standstill after a hundred and fifty days at sea. Pemberton had arrived downriver on a flat-bottomed lighter two days before, so he would have no idea as to the profound relief of simply stopping. Lacing his fingers around the rail, Augustus held on tightly, a surge of people below now spreading out across the dock.

He could smell fire and oil and grease, and the wind

from the city carried other less palatable scents. Fish was being unloaded somewhere close, the rancid oiliness making his stomach turn. The sharper smell of livestock was there, too.

Captain McAdams was beside him, his voice loud with an authority befitting his position.

'I can take you down, for a carriage has been ordered and your luggage will follow. St James's Square, is it not, Mr Rushworth? Your factor said he had arranged it.'

'Very well.'

The wind seemed to heighten on this side of the ship as he followed the Captain to a gangplank bridging the dark, cold water below and he jammed his hat further down on his head.

Three women were standing under an open-sided wooden structure ten yards away from where the gangplank met the dock, an older woman and two younger ones. The older woman's voice was laced with irritation.

'I should have known this whole trip to see the Frost Fair was a foolish one, Mia, and now we are marooned here till another conveyance can be found and my cough is becoming worse and worse by the moment.'

The smaller woman she spoke to wore an oversized hat allowing no glimpse of her face from this angle, but her voice was arresting.

'It is of no significance at all, Mama,' she said, a slice of desperation easily heard in the words. 'Why, I shall find transport before you know it and then we shall all be whipped off home, you to a glass or two of the sherry you enjoy and Susan to a hot bath. Just wait and see. It will be accomplished in a moment and we will be as warm as toast before a blazing fire and this adventure of exploring the Frost Fair shall be behind us.'

But the mama was having none of it. 'This adventure, as you call it, is one that has afforded me no pleasure at all, so please do stop pretending it has. It is simply far too cold to be out and about and the people here are vulgar—and that is before mentioning the ever-present danger of falling through the ice.'

The bigger woman swayed then and both girls stepped forward to help her, though her bulky frame leaned more heavily on the thinner one who had just spoken.

'Do you need somewhere to sit perhaps...?'

She looked around then and in doing so a face as perfect as anything Augustus had ever seen in his whole life came into view, bright blue eyes searching until they alighted on his own, wide in shock, glinting with worry.

She held up the older woman by sheer dint of courage, her arms shaking with the endeavour, sweat even in the cold of this day gleaming above her shapely upper lip.

He walked forward. 'Take mine.'

'You are offering us your carriage, sir?'

Up close, he saw freckles across the bridge of her nose and deep dimples etched in each cheek. Not in humour, but in clenching and unnerving consternation.

Nodding, he used one arm to gesture them in. 'Indeed I am.'

'Well, we should not wish to inconvenience you, but this kind offer is one we are unable to refuse because

Mama is feeling so ill and if we tarry I am not certain we should ever find another—'

Her words were cut off entirely as the older woman she held slumped against her, the full weight knocking her off balance. Within a breath, Augustus was there, steadying the younger woman and lifting the older one into the carriage seat behind them.

The blue-eyed daughter pushed in even before he had finished, flattening herself against him, the scent of lemon and flowers making him turn.

'I am sorry, but her skirt has slipped up and her stockings are all on show…' Deftly replacing the skirts around her mother's legs, she pulled at her hat. He could see no familial resemblance at all between them, though he could clearly see one in the other young woman. 'Mama would be mortified by anything vulgar and as such it behoves me to make sure that even in this state she is exactly as she would want to be. I know you would understand that, sir, a feminine nonsense, I suppose, but important nonetheless.'

He turned away from all these words, slipping and sliding over the explanation, filling in each and every moment. Did the dimpled girl never stop talking? He could not quite place motive on such verbosity, but she was not finished, no, not by a long shot.

'If you would allow me your name and furnish us with your direction, we will of course reimburse such a kindness and make certain you are repaid for the trouble. Mama has the purse, you see, deep in her pocket, and I don't like to trouble her to find it in this state.' On looking around, he saw her brow furrow. 'It might be a while, you understand, before another carriage can be procured for the docks are busy today with all the traffic, though we will send this one back to you the moment we are at home and home is not far, sir, of that fact I can assure you.'

Augustus shook his head, wishing she would go, wishing he could go, wishing with every single fibre of his being that a long and lengthy argument would not now be needed in order to send her on her way.

The other daughter solved the problem when she called out, fearing her mother was going to be sick.

Blue eyes raked across him, wide in consternation. 'I am so very sorry.'

Five words ended it. In the next second she was gone, the door shut behind her, the driver calling out for the horses to move forward. There was a clatter of hooves on timber, the whoosh of movement and then the stillness of absence.

He had given her none of his personal details and had received none in return. He had no idea at all of who she was and no way to find out either, but his day had changed in a way he could not quite fathom— inexorably and finally.

'God.' He said this beneath his breath, the acknowledgement of shock unsettling. The older lady had called her Mia. Was that her name or was it short for something else? She had said her home was not far and while her accent had been that of a genteel lady, her clothes were decidedly worn.

* * *

Miss Euphemia Denniston sat bolt upright in the seat of the borrowed conveyance as the distance between herself and the dockyards widened.

He was beautiful in a dark, raw and brooding way, this stranger, his largeness allowing him to lift her stepmother into her seat as if she were a mere feather. He had scars across the fingers of his right hand, significant old scars that spoke of some accident—she had seen them up close as she had pushed past him—and his voice was tinged with an accent that was not quite English.

An outsider. From somewhere far away. She knew his ship had come in from across the seas for the sails had the look of storms and time and miles.

She wished she might simply turn around and stare, but she knew she was far too old for such impossible imaginings.

'I wonder who our saviour was, Mama.' Her stepsister's question was sharp. 'He lifted you without any problem at all and his clothes were most fine. Did you not think they were, Mia?'

In truth, Mia had barely noticed the clothes of which Susan spoke. She had been too focused on his eyes. Obsidian. A blackish brown with no light in them at all. Hard eyes full of the competence and arrogance that she had always steered well clear of in a man.

Her stepmother mulled over the question.

'He hardly spoke, Susan, and did not appear to want to either, though he did indeed look most well.'

Lucille had recovered a little now and the paleness in her cheeks was less noticeable; the directness that was far more like her had returned.

'Perhaps it was the cold that disconcerted you, Mama? Are you warm enough?'

'I am now, though I think I shall take to my bed for a few days just to make sure of no ongoing ill effects. Perhaps you might ask the driver the name of the stranger, Mia, so that we could at least thank him?'

'Of course.' Euphemia's anxiety rose and with a sigh she turned away to the window. 'It will snow soon, for the clouds are low and purple. It will be a good thing for the fair as the ice will not melt as quickly.'

The weather was an easier subject to speak of, something unremarkable and ordinary. She needed that for she felt unsettled and on the edge of something different, a perception of falling and falling as if she had lost balance, a dizzy desire that was unfamiliar replacing her more usual rational sense.

Ridiculous, she chastised herself, but could not get rid of the sensation. If she had been alone she might have burst into tears, which was even more surprising given that she very rarely cried.

Who was he?

The words echoed around each part of her as she tried to remember everything about their odd meeting. He had worn boots to the knee, boots fastened with silver buttons—she had noticed these as he had come down the gangplank—and he had been tall, much taller than she was. His hair had been worn brushed back, more as a way of getting it out of his eyes than for any statement of fashion, and it had been as dark as night.

A man of shadows and silence.

He'd smelt of spices, Mia thought then, reaching for the memory—cinnamon, perhaps, or nutmeg—and around his wrist he'd worn a silver bracelet engraved with curious markings that she had not recognised.

A stranger. Stranger even with the recall. He did not fit a pattern or meld into the shape of any society men she'd seen. Such fancy made her frown and her step-mother caught the movement.

'Well, at least we are almost home, and I am so relieved that I don't think I shall venture out again until this freeze thaws.'

'There is the Allans' ball, Mama,' Susan said. It was in four days' time. 'Perhaps the gentleman we just met might be attending.'

There was a note in her stepsister's voice that was different. At twenty, Susan was a beautiful girl with many admirers, but thus far had indicated no intention of settling down with any of them. Could she be interested in this one?

Lucille, wanting to placate Susan's worry, relented. 'I am sure that things will look very differently then than they do now, my dear. If you feel the need to go, then of course we should and Euphemia can accompany us as a companion in case of further problems, for my poor health is beginning to worry me and I should not wish to be caught out. The dark blue gown we procured last year will suffice for such an event, Mia, as at your age there is very little chance of any suitor approaching you and we have no money for a new one.'

Euphemia's heart sank at the mention of the ball and of her stepmother's expectation of her attending it. 'The blue gown will be more than acceptable.'

Privately she wondered if Lucille had truly ever looked at the garment. It had come to her second-hand through a friend of the family and even then had required extensive stitching to hide the considerable wear and tear.

But her stepmother was right in another respect. She had had her time in society nearly fourteen years ago and it had been a disaster. Subsequently, she had accepted her position within the family of her father's second marriage without question, knowing any further hopes for a different future were futile and pointless.

There would be no knight in shining armour riding into her life to whisk her off to paradise, no second chances, given what had happened with the first. Shaking that thought away, she watched as the conveyance drew up before their house, the belt of sleet-driven rain finally reducing to a fine cold mist.

A moment later, she approached the driver as he stood by the horses. The man was checking a strap on one side of the harness and tightening it.

'My mother would like to thank the gentleman who allowed us the use of this conveyance. I know you are going back to retrieve their party, but before you go, could you allow me his name and direction?'

The driver shook his head even as he smiled at her.

'The carriage was organised a few days ago, miss, and we were simply told to wait on that particular dock when the ship was due to berth. I just go along with the instructions and make sure we are there at the time stated.'

'I see.'

She stood back and watched as he took his place on the box seat and called the horses on. There was no way they would find out the stranger's name; she just had to accept the fact. As she hurried inside, the coldness of the day made her shiver.

Augustus undid his neckcloth and threw it on the chair beside the bed, then he removed his jacket. Numerous fires had been set around the town house and the temperature in his room was almost cloying. Outside, snow fell, the threat of it all day finally materialising, and the park opposite was soon coated in white.

Mr Thomas Pemberton had eventually left, something he was concerned might never happen as his grandfather's factor had insisted on showing him every room of the property in detail. He remembered the place, of course he did, but he had only been here three or four times in his youth and had not liked it much.

His hands covered his eyes, pushing at a headache that was becoming worse as he thought of his grandfather. The old Baron was cranky and irritable, but he hadn't been immoral or weak. It was Augustus's father and brother who had picked up those mantles and fashioned them as their own.

'Lord,' he muttered to himself. England brought out the worst in him. He'd only come back because his father's recent death had left a hole in the family order of inheritance, a hole that his grandfather wanted addressed, and as the title would come to Augustus next it was difficult to refuse such a summons.

Twirling the silver bracelet at his wrist, he read the message within it, remembering. He could hear the wind rising and the sleet hammering against glass, thickening the ice on the river, no doubt, and putting paid to any outside activity.

The blue-eyed girl he'd helped today came to mind. He hoped she was tucked in with her family somewhere warm and safe. He wished he'd known her name, but they had not waited for the carriage to return, the factor having procured another with more ease than expected. Perhaps he should have tarried and asked the first driver her address? That thought made him frown and he dismissed it.

Euphemia regarded the hustle and bustle of London through her window—the lights, the outlines of the city, the last traffic hurrying home in the snow.

Releasing her hair, she drew her fingers through the heaviness of it and closed her eyes.

Alone. Finally.

She'd talked too much today in her encounter with the man at the dock, she knew she had, but nerves always made her verbose and years in the company of her stepmother and stepsister after the death of her father had only added to the habit.

She was here only by the good grace of Lucille and she had learned through harder moments that the way of ingratiation was in familiarity, endearments, good humour and positivity.

Keep it light. Keep chatting. Allow no one at all to know how you felt. The truth was a dangerous enemy and unless Lucille saw her as an utterly indispensable member of this household she had very few other options.

Her father had been rescued from bankruptcy by his marriage and everyone in the family knew it: her stepmother, her stepsister and her father with his increasingly heavy bouts of despondency and drinking. Lucille Hitchkins may have come with some money, but she had also come with a tight fist and after a disastrous Season of coming out in London, Mia had been allowed back only under duress. Another mouth to feed. A further expense. An ageing stepdaughter who would not attract a glorious union. A burden.

But Mia would not think about that.

She was here and would have to make the best of it; there were many other women in London in her position who were a lot worse off. She had a home, food and warmth, and her father had impressed upon her again and again in the last months of his life that she must be grateful for her lot.

In truth she was appreciative, for Lucille was not the stepmother of the stories which abounded, the cold-hearted cruel witch who locked her unwanted relation in a garret and threw her a crust of bread now and then.

No, she was not that and, although she was a woman of moods and inclined to be sulky, she had risen to her responsibilities under difficult circumstances and allowed Mia a place in her home.

Her own mistakes were a part of those trials, too, she acknowledged; her foolishness at the Dashwoods' ball had caused all that followed, the imprudent and unwise decisions she had made which had cost her everything.

The very thought of it made her feel sick, but, although she still did not enjoy partaking in the bigger society events, she knew she would need to attend the Allans' ball. Going over to the wardrobe, she pulled out her navy gown and held it up against herself in the mirror.

The colour suited her hair and brought out the blue in her eyes. It might be old, but it was well made, the fabric of a fine quality and the stitching even.

A thought made her hesitate and, opening the drawer at the bottom of her nightstand, she brought out a plain wooden box. Inside was the only thing she had of her mother's: a double-stranded pearl necklace with an intricate clasp of gold. She had seldom worn it for fear of Susan wanting to borrow the piece and then losing it, so it had been tucked up in its cotton bed for years.

Draping the necklace across the navy gown, Mia looked at herself, at the hope in her eyes and at the sadness.

'This is who you have become,' she whispered to her reflection. 'This woman who hides things.'

She imagined a mother she had never met fastening the pearls around her neck. Were her eyes blue? Was her hair fair? Was she small and pale, too? Her father had never talked of her real mama and any questions she'd had were always rebuffed by him. She had never seen a drawn likeness, or a journal containing personal thoughts, though she would have dearly loved both.

The most her father had ever told her was that her mother, Elizabeth Anne-Marie Caughey, had been prudent and judicious. He'd also said that she had not made any fuss at all as she had died, slipping off to her death the evening after Euphemia was born with barely a whisper.

Mia's fingers slid across the pearls and she felt their smoothness. There had been no other living relatives to ask and so she had had to make do with only these few, small sentences. When she was younger she had imagined her father to have been so distraught about her mother's death that he could not bring himself to mention her name again, but as she had grown older she'd seen other things.

He didn't care. He was happy to forget. For him, moving on was all that was important and, when Mrs Lucille Hitchkins, an attractive young widow of means with a very young daughter in tow, had caught his eye, he had taken his chance and married her.

Mia clutched the pearls tighter. Her father's second marriage had probably been about as successful as his first, a lack of love and true discourse having been apparent from the very beginning. It had taken less than two years for him to spend large tracts of time away from the family, including her, and when he did return she could see his disappointment.

He never shouted or hit out or argued, he just drank in silence and in solitude, and when the liquor finally killed him, Lucille had buried him without fanfare and carried on.

Like she herself was doing now, Mia thought. Making the best of a bad situation and carrying on.

Except, for the first time in a long while she felt different and such an alteration had a lot to do with the man she had seen on the docks today with his dark eyes and hair.

She had been just seventeen when she had been persuaded into the corridor by the young Mr Rushworth and most unprepared for betrayal. She was thirty now, a spinster without the illusion that something better would come along. If her instincts then had been poor, now they were bound up with rock-solid sense and no-nonsense practicality.

As prudent and old-fashioned as her name. Discreet. Pragmatic. Sensible. Like her mother had been.

She would never marry. No, she would get on with life and be thankful for the small comforts she had been allotted and for a place within a household that kept her safe. Putting away both the necklace and the gown, she chose a book from the shelf on one side of the room and made herself ready for bed.

But the events of the day still tumbled in, the sound of the stranger's voice, the darkness of his eyes, the feel of his hand at her elbow...

A man who looked dangerous and intractable. A man who would not bow to her bidding like her pliant night-time dream lover. A man as far from her idea of ease and comfort as she might ever imagine. A man to avoid and be wary of. She hoped with all her heart that he would not be at the Allans' ball.

Augustus had always walked at night, but London had a different feel to it than Bombay. The climate, of course, was one such variance, but there were also myriad other disparities. It no longer felt like home, for one. No, now the city was foreign and threatening, the poverty and the anger tumbling from the broken back-streets almost palpable. There was an emptiness here, a desolation that no one solution might remedy. India had its poverty, too, but it was a gentler version, religion softening the edges of disparity.

He couldn't go back though, for his time there was past, gone and finished with. It was just that this void held a dread that made him falter—something he very rarely did—his pathways thus far having been well determined and well-travelled.

The mist was rising, cold and certain, blurring the outlines of the buildings and lending a silence to the drenched city streets, but at least the snow had abated. He wanted the discomfort, wanted the cold to cut into his skin and make him feel…anything, for this noth-ingness was unbearable.

A noise behind made him turn as three men came up behind him. Big men, rough men, men with the look of both danger and stupidity mixed together in that singular fashion of misguided intent.

'Give us over your purse, guv, and you can be on your way.'

The fellow next to him sniggered. 'On his way to the afterlife, more like.'

Augustus lifted his hands before him in the age-old gesture of defence.

'I'd advise you to move on, gentlemen. I'm not looking for a fight.'

'Is that so then, guv…?' The first man took a large knife from his pocket and held it balanced carefully, the jagged blade pointed towards him. The others had knives, too, their silver edges caught in the moonlight.

He went in low, catching the first thief's legs and taking him to ground, heartened by the heavy sound of a head against cobbles. The next man was easier again. A simple turn of his arm and he heard a crack of bone. The third man also heard it; his face disbelieving, he dropped the knife, which turned over and over in the light until it landed, the water of the gutter spilling across metal, dark and slippery. Like blood.

There was only the sound of heavy boots now running across the emptiness, a retreat that was welcomed as Augustus stood and brushed himself down, retrieving his hat from the street and jamming it on his head.

They would have headaches and worse come the morning, these rapscallions, he was sure of it. Kicking the blade into a pile of rubbish, he walked away, listening now for the return of any others and making sure that he was not followed.

One corner and then two more. He backtracked down Piccadilly and walked across to Green Park, into the darkness, leaning against a tree finally and feeling its sturdiness.

India had held its own dangers but the army of the East India Company had taught him how to survive. At first he'd been a green boy, prone to accident and injury, but after a year he'd understood the stillness needed in defence and the quickness in attack. He'd killed people in the service of the army there, but it had been years since he had needed to resort to such a final blow.

Running his fingers through his hair, he pushed at the aching muscles in his neck and listened to his heart beating like a drum. So many days at sea had left him soft, like his father, he reflected then, but he banished such a thought.

Family. His own reflection made him shudder. He needed a drink and he needed company and White's was just around the next corner at the top of St James's.

The place was full when he got there, every room across the two floors alight. As luck would have it, one of his best friends from school, the Honourable Bramwell Baker-Hill, was sitting at the first table in the lounge and he called him over.

'August, I thought never to see you again after you left so suddenly. It is so good to have you back.' His eyes took in the wet patches on his coat. 'Have you been caught in the rain?'

'I was waylaid in Shepherd Street by three thugs.'

'My God. Did they hurt you?'

'No. They left quickly when they knew I did not intend to empty my pockets as they had asked.'

'Hell, what is England coming to?'

Bram poured generous drinks into two glasses as he spoke and beckoned Augustus to the chair opposite. 'When did you get home?'

'Just today after a long sea voyage.'

'As the new and improved heir to the Rushworth title?'

Augustus looked up quickly, the tone of his friend's voice at odds with the sentiment.

'I know he was your father, but he was a bore and a cheat. I heard it said that the women of London society breathed a sigh of relief when he passed, his wandering eye blamed for a vast number of shocking scandals in bed as well as out.'

Augustus made himself hold still. The truth of the family evil had not percolated into gossip then, for these memories were only benign things, the wayward wanderings of a lusty lord. Society could stomach and forgive such tendencies as the red-blooded failings of excess. It was his brother's flaws that they would never condone.

He took the glass Bram offered him and almost emptied it, the smooth brandy exactly what he needed.

'We missed you, for God's sake. You didn't even say goodbye.'

'Well, it was a spur-of-the-moment decision to leave and the tide was kind.'

'Kind enough to allow escape?'

Bramwell had always been the most perceptive of his friends.

'I'm back to stay. I just want…peace, Bram.'

"'Peace? I hate the word as I hate Hell and all Montagues."'

Augustus laughed at the recited verse and remembered why they had been such good friends.

'The Capulets were angels and innocents compared to my family.'

'I know.'

And that was it. A settling. A resolution. For this moment, England and his position here looked more certain than it had in years and a warmth began to distil through the coldness.

'Who else knows you are back?'

'My grandfather. He sent for me.'

'The prodigal grandson?'

Augustus ignored that.

'I heard you were married out there in India?'

'I was, but my wife died.'

'Then I am sorry for it.'

'Thank you.'

Bram poured another drink and for a second they

both simply sat there, the mirth in the club swirling around them and far from anything they'd spoken of thus far.

'Word is you've made a fortune in Bombay with the East India Company?'

'Well, the building of an empire is not without its risks for trade and politics make uneasy bed companions. But, yes, raw cotton and spices are always easy to sell no matter which port they are dispatched to or from, and I dispatched a lot of them.'

Bram frowned. 'I wish I'd gone with you when you left, August, though I am married now and have a daughter.'

'A daughter?' Augustus's heart skipped a beat. 'What is her name?'

'Catherine, but we call her Kit. She is six years old.'

Alice. The name swam in grief as he looked down at the bracelet he always wore, one finger rubbing at the markings.

'A fine life then, by the sounds of it. A life that makes sense?'

'I suppose that is true. Come to the Allans' ball on Tuesday, August. Rupert Forsythe will be there and Tobias Balcombe as well, though Tony Ferris is up visiting his ailing mother in Oxford and not expected back for a week or so. They'll all be thrilled to see you.'

Augustus finished his drink, the names of old friends from another lifetime ago making him wonder if he had the guts to try to reclaim it all over again.

'Perhaps I will come.' The words were drawn in uncertainty.

'I hope you do. Now, tell me about the East India Company and Bombay. I've heard such things about the place that I can barely believe to be true and Lance Sedgwick returned last year with stories of grandness and excess. He will be there on Tuesday as well so undoubtedly will want your time.'

The exalted world of English society came back, the world that once had been his own, many years ago, a world of balls and manners and etiquette.

Could he fit in again? Would he want to?

The darkness that sat on his shoulders seemed heavier than usual as he smiled and made himself listen to Bram telling him of all that had once been and now was not.

The next day, a steady stream of visitors presented themselves at the town house in St James's, his mother's sister included, and she arrived with Lady Langham and her twenty-year-old daughter in tow.

'I could not believe you were home, Rushworth, after all these years, and the rumours that are buzzing around have it that you are here to stay. Why, Lady Langham was just saying you must allow us all to show you the many changes in the city and her oldest daughter, Miss Annabelle, would be most pleased to point out the new landmarks from the perspective of a younger person.'

Miss Annabelle Langham nodded, her dark curls

bouncing up and down, a look on her face that was worrying.

'I am certain you will be amazed at the changes, Mr Rushworth, and it must be very different from India. It is just such a shame that you have arrived on one of the very coldest days of the season, though at least it is not as foggy as it has been.'

The young woman's voice was careful and carried the sort of accent his wife had perfected, one with a good deal of practised art and sultriness within it.

His aunt took up the subject with relish. 'Your mother would have been delighted that you are no longer languishing so far from home and, after all the sad losses your family have endured, your grandfather must be relieved to have an heir back in the country who is whole, hearty and hale. I do hope you might grace the balls of the Season, too, Rushworth. Why, Annabelle here is one of the originals this year and would be happy to partner you to any of the larger occasions given you are so newly back. There is a small soirée at the Taits' tomorrow and another one at the Digbys' the night after...'

Augustus stopped her. 'I think I will settle in first before I venture back into the melee of society. But I thank you for the offer and will undoubtedly see you at the Allans' ball.'

Such a blatant request was vulgar and unwanted, but he did not feel up to the fuss of a refusal. The young Miss Annabelle Langham looked at him in a way that made him feel cagey, for this was a society that took even the smallest word as an affirmation for something so much more and acted upon it. He was aggravated at his aunt's obvious collusion with the Langhams, too, and when she beamed and tucked her arm through his he felt even more annoyed. She had never been an easy woman and had made no effort with him as a young boy, favouring Jeremy instead in that ingratiating way of hers.

If his mother had been anything like her youngest sister, he could almost understand his father's lack of love.

'Will the Baron be coming down to London to welcome you back, Rushworth?'

'I doubt it. He is said to prefer the north.'

'He is at Amerleigh House?' Lady Langham breathed the words, her eyes alight at the mention. 'We went there once many years ago to a party and I have always said that the place is one of the most magnificent estates in all of England. You must long to be back there, Mr Rushworth?'

'Must I?'

He knew such an answer was barely civil, but he had had enough of these guests—people he did not like and did not want here with all their airs and graces. His aunt frowned as he stepped away.

'I am sorry, but you have caught me at a difficult time and I am late for an appointment.'

'Then we will take our leave, but shall expect to see you at the Allans' ball.'

When they had gone, Augustus instructed his butler to tell any other visitors that he was not at home because he did not want a repeat of that awful meeting. There were dozens of mamas in London needing a wealthy and marriageable man for their daughters and he was the newest offering. That thought made him swear.

When the doorbell sounded a few moments later, he couldn't believe it. Surely they could not be back?

Then a familiar voice made him smile. Tobias Balcombe. Augustus strode through the house to greet him and just in time, for Higgins was trying to send him on his way.

'Tobias.'

Dark green eyes blazed as his friend moved forward. 'Bram told me you were back half an hour ago and I had to come and see for myself that such a thing was true.' Warm arms wrapped around him. 'When the hell did you arrive?'

'Yesterday on the midday tide and on the coldest day I can ever remember.'

'It's been below freezing every night since Christmas, August, and the ice on the Thames is thick enough to hold a Frost Fair.'

'I know. I came in to the middle of it.'

'Who else have you seen apart from Bramwell?'

'No one.'

'Was that not Miss Annabelle Langham and her mother I just noticed leaving? I will give you a word of warning to take care there, August, unless you want to be married forthwith. The daughter may be beautiful, but she is also undeniably desperate to snag a worthy groom. Bram said you'd had a wife?'

'I did, but she died two years ago. She was born in India and was the daughter of a colonel in the East India Company operating out of Bombay.'

'Then I hope you might find some happiness back here. Perhaps you might consider settling near us.'

'Us?'

'I am happily married now, August, and I have three children of eight, six and two.'

'Bram told me of his own family last night.'

'After you left so unexpectedly, it felt like the wild exploits of our youth were less attractive. We had all settled down within two years of you going and sometimes when we met we spoke of the fact that it was you who was probably the cause of that. It seemed to all of us that if life and friendship could be lost so easily it was time to set down roots. We missed you, though I never could understand why you had not found the time to say goodbye, for it wouldn't have taken much to let us know.'

The past reached out to claim him—the hurt, the blood, the betrayals. He turned his hand over and looked at the scars there and knew that this was just a small part of the picture. But he could not reveal the truth of why he had left. He could not say that his unhinged brother had tried to kill him, in cold blood, in the middle of the afternoon, and it was only a miracle that he had survived it.

Instead he placed a hand over Tobias's. 'I am back now.'

'And I am glad for it.'

Chapter Two

Mia placed her pearls carefully under the collar of her navy gown, tucking the double strand in so that the clasp would not inadvertently loosen.

She appeared presentable, she thought, as she took one last look at herself in the mirror, presentable not in the way of a young girl who had all the dreams of a romantic night in her eyes, but in a sturdy, sensible sort of way that spoke of fortitude and wisdom. A woman who was armed with the flat realisation that the world was neither a safe nor a kind place and would tread carefully wherever she went.

Her sister joined her at the top of the staircase, her new gown one of tawny gold and shimmering in the light.

'You look beautiful, Susan. I am sure you will be the belle of the ball this evening.'

'I hope it is not too much.' Her fingers pulled at the skirt, smoothing it down. 'The fabric was a good price when Mama and I first saw it, but now I think it was because it's rather…loud?'

'It's lovely and Mr Kevin Allan will notice you immediately and be smitten.' Euphemia had had plenty of practice reassuring her stepsister, and although to her eyes the fabric did look rather sparkly, at this late hour she knew it was much better not to say anything.

'Well, I was hoping that the stranger we met the other day at the docks might attend. What must it be like to dance with a man like that? Such masculinity has an attraction that cannot be denied, don't you think? Do you imagine he might be wealthy as well and have a whole string of houses to his name?'

A slight anger surfaced at such a reply. 'I have no idea whatsoever. One piece of advice I would give you, though, is to be wary of men such as that, Susan. You are young, with all of your dreams in front of you, and sometimes temptations can be dangerous.'

'Dangerous?'

'We know nothing of him. His family. His circumstances. His character.'

As she said the words, Euphemia could hear her inner voice countering her words.

Remember your temptations? Did you stand back and wait for a confirmation of character when you were Susan's age?

She was relieved when Lucille joined them in the blue salon, for all talk of the man they had met at the docks ceased. Her sister, at least, had enough caution for that.

'Gold suits you entirely, my darling girl, just as Madame Blanc said it would, and the cut of the gown makes you look so elegant.' Lucille was effusive in her compliments. 'Our carriage will be here in a few moments, but I thought we could have a sherry to warm our bones before we go. Mia, will you go and find some from the room next door and bring it to us for I have something of import to say?'

'Of course.'

A few moments later, Euphemia had poured them all a glass and Lucille raised hers most formally.

'The good news is that your aunt in Bath has asked us to stay for a few weeks.'

Susan's gasp of delight stopped her mother momentarily.

'She has offered to sponsor you, my dear, into an appearance at the great salons and has assured me that the quality of the people there is beyond reproach. She invites me as well, to keep her company, so we would make a jolly party of three.'

'And what of Mia? Will she come, too?' Her stepsister's loyalty was warming.

'No, for she will stay here and make sure the house runs smoothly. We shall be back in twelve days and will tell her all about it. I hardly think she would want to be a part of such an endeavour at her age, do not you agree, Euphemia?'

'Of course.' Mia tried to temper her words, but delight ran rampant. Twelve days by herself to do exactly as she wished: to read, to walk, to eat meals she enjoyed in the places she desired. It was a gift of great magnitude and the night picked up in a way she would never have expected.

'The gowns we have procured for you here in London, Susan, will do very well for our Bath sojourn so we shall be leaving here in three days' time. While we are away, Euphemia, you might take the opportunity to make certain the house receives a thorough clean for it certainly needs it. We shall leave the cook and the kitchen lad here and take the two other maids to help us.'

'Of course.'

'You have never liked society much, Mia, so perhaps it will be a relief for you?' Susan's words were gentler than her mother's.

'It will be, indeed, and I hope you will have a wonderful time in Bath.'

The Allans' town house was brimming with lights and movement: the departing and arriving carriages, the drivers in their livery, the guests in their warm winter cloaks hurrying up the wide front staircase, laughing and chattering. Mia's heart had already started to race and she employed her usual trick of calming herself, counting the people, listing the colours, adding up the candles set in glass as they made their way into the house.

Inside, it was just as busy—three large salons all open to each other and a band playing on a raised stage set up between the first and second rooms.

The colour of the night was yellow. The servants all had yellow satin jackets and the walls and windows were draped in the same shade. It was like sunshine after the dark coldness of the night outside.

For years after the Dashwoods' ball, Euphemia had not attended a single social event, but after enough time had passed she had been pulled back in a measured way. The dreadful Mr Rushworth had unexpectedly died four or so years after her encounter with him and she could not help feeling relief at the certainty of never meeting him again. She said a prayer for his soul even as she thought this, though a less than charitable anger still remained in her heart, even now.

People crowded in around them after they had been received by the hosts who stood at a line at the door. Mr Kevin Allan had appeared genuinely taken by Susan's appearance and had left the receiving line to join their party.

'Will you save a dance for me, Miss Denniston, when the music begins? If I don't ask now, I fear I might miss out altogether.'

Susan demurred and brought out her dance card and the young suitor filled in two spaces, both waltzes, his smile wide and hopeful.

'It's rather a crush here tonight, I'm afraid, but my mother is particularly pleased with the attendance of many of those well up the social ladder who happen to be in town this early in the year.'

'Is she?' Lucille asked this with a sort of simmering excitement that made Mia cringe. She had forgotten how very in awe her stepmother was of those with any sort of a title. It was why she had married Mia's father in the first place, for his grandfather had been an honourable from up north.

As Mr Allan began to point out different people in the huge room, Mia's eyes wandered around the edges to watch those grouped before the rows of pillars draped in bright greenery.

So many people were already in attendance and others still arriving. Although the Season hadn't really started, more of society than usual was in London on account of the Frost Fairs. She felt the excitement all around her and the laughter of friends and acquaintances, an easy affability and openness that was completely at odds with her own stiff uncertainty. She knew no one here, save her stepmother and stepsister, and they were both fully immersed in the joviality of the occasion and trying to impress the young Mr Allan. She slowed her breathing, counting out the beats as she drew in air, holding it in and then letting it out. Four in, five held and eight out. The numbers never altered; they were a constant against her stress, a way to cope.

Mia's smile stiffened and she took another sip of the orange cordial she had been offered. Blending in was as much of an art as standing out, she decided— the world you formed around you allowed a disappearance that was safe.

No one glanced at her with interest, no one came forward. She was a plain and impoverished relative, disregarded and relegated to the forgotten pile. Such a

position suited her here in society and she had perfected
the role since Susan had been brought out five months
ago. She was a chaperon. A woman who stood to one
side, watching. Not a wallflower because they at least
hoped for a dance or a chance of flirtation, whereas she
most definitely did not.

The crowd had momentarily fallen silent, which
was unusual, and the name of a guest rang through
the crowd as the major-domo's voice introduced the
next arrival.

'Mr Rushworth of Cheshire.'

Rushworth? Here? Returned from the dead and alive?
She held on to the stem of her glass so hard her hand
began to shake and she made herself stop. He had died
years ago, surely, a scandal that involved a duel at his
family seat in Cheshire. The details had never been
made public, but there were whispers of hidden motives and undisclosed disgrace.

She felt sick while the world about her floated away,
a dizzy horror making her lose both breath and balance.
Rushworth? Here tonight? It could not possibly be…

A tall, dark-haired man appeared at the top of the
stairs. Beautifully dressed, his clothes showed off a figure that spoke of physical exercise and hard effort. But
it was his face that arrested her.

It was the stranger from the dock, with all his beauty
and darkness and mystery.

'Mr Rushworth of Amerleigh House?' This excla-
mation came from somewhere close by and Mia heard
the surprise erupt all around her and saw the looks on

the faces of the ladies. Fierce, wanting looks. Calculated, hungry looks. Looks that told of desire and longing and need.

Her stranger had transformed into this new man, who had a laughing demeanour as he greeted those surrounding him, easy in company, relaxed in himself.

A beautiful young woman was on his arm now, hanging on for all she was worth, her eyes knowing, her certainty apparent. Others were there, too, questioning him, calling to him, the cream of society welcoming back the grandson of a baron into their fold of privilege.

'He's been away for all of ten years,' she heard the man behind her say.

'And he has made a fortune,' another added, 'and brought it back with him to find a bride.'

'Well, he'll have no trouble whatsoever,' said yet another. 'Look at the way Miss Annabelle Langham is hanging on to his arm, and she is the very cream of this Season.'

Every hope that Mia had harboured of this being an ordinary night shattered and fell in tiny shards of sharpness all around her. He was the darling of English society and he was the brother of the man who had taken her into a darkened corridor at the Dashwood ball all those years before and hurt her.

A whim. A dalliance. A small and unimportant flirtation with a girl who had been foolish enough not to understand what was happening. If she closed her eyes she was there again, his sweating body pushing up against her own even as she told him no, his fingers bruising…

She shook her head and took a breath, trying to regain her nonchalance even as a pernicious nausea surfaced.

'My goodness,' her stepmother said suddenly. 'Look. Is that not the same man who offered us his carriage at the dock on the day of the Frost Fair?'

Mia nodded because she did not trust her voice. She could only stand there in shock and stupor.

Tonight he was different. His hair, for a start, was left loose and was curling at his nape, the collar of a snowy white neckcloth accentuating both the darkness and the length.

She didn't want to meet him, didn't want him to see her like this, with her hair tightened flat and oily against her skull and a gown that was nowhere near its best. The pearls seemed like a mistake, too, their radiance and richness out of place at her collar, a small vanity that she should not have allowed herself, given both her position and her advanced age.

They were outdated and archaic. She felt so past her prime at the moment that she wished she could have disappeared, been anywhere but in this crowded room, her lonely maturity unbecoming and sad.

Turning, she tried to concentrate on the words Mr Allan was giving her sister, sweet words of admiration and regard, but a rushing nervousness made everything difficult as she noted in which direction Mr Rushworth walked and with whom he talked. At least he did not venture in her direction, but seemed to be striking off to the next salon, a great number of people trailing in his wake.

'I don't believe we will get to speak with the young Mr Rushworth, for he is very much in demand. A pity that, for I have no doubt he would remember us.' Lucille watched him like a hawk might a field mouse.

Mia had no such certitude. 'He looks busy, Mama, and the young lady at his side is holding on tightly to him.'

Her stepmother made a point of looking at Susan and then across to the beautiful woman Mia had mentioned.

'Yes, perhaps now is not a good time, after all— besides, Susan is doing very well with her young suitor as it is.'

Just at that moment, Rushworth glanced up and saw them watching him. In consternation, Mia tore her eyes away, the horror of him catching them both observing him making her grit her teeth together.

Damn, she thought. She wished she could go home, but it was still early and any unexplained withdrawal would be met with questions later. Her only hope was that he would not recognise her, her age rendering her barely visible and their meeting on the docks having been most brief.

His party had stopped near the pillars that separated the rooms now, more and more people joining them. His height was striking because she could see his head well above the crowd, a smile on his face and a stillness that she had noted the day she'd first met him. She watched him again now only at intervals, making ready to pull her eyes away from the group in case he looked back as she tried to listen to the conversation around her, but the room was hot and the noise was loud and all she wanted to do was escape.

'You need to smile more, Euphemia,' her stepmother was saying. 'People will think you have just come from a funeral and it is most off-putting. Sometimes I wonder why we even bother with you.'

'Of course.' Her throat tightened and her anxiety rose, but not wanting to attract any attention she made an excuse to refresh herself, a timely retreat that would allow her a moment alone.

Away from the crowd, she took in a breath and tried to collect herself, struggling to remember all the ways she had learned to survive. The breathing. The stillness. The calm.

It would be all right. She could get through this. Mr Rushworth would not remember her from the docks, she was sure of it, but she still had the worry of her stepmother approaching him and she prayed fervently that Lucille would not.

Sitting in an alcove a few moments later, hidden behind a large plant, and relishing the time alone, Mia heard people join her, giggles and breathless joviality entering the quiet space.

'I told you Mr Rushworth would be here tonight, Emily, and is he not a thousand times more handsome than the stories of him say?'

'Annabelle Langham has not let him go since his

arrival and, knowing her as we do, she will not for the entire night.'

'He's richer than anyone else in the room and has a grandfather who is ancient and titled.'

'Did you see Miss Susan Denniston eyeing him up? Surely she does not think she holds a chance?'

'Well, she is beautiful, is she not, in a dark sort of way, though the family surrounding her tonight look most out of sorts. Have you ever seen a dress as old and shabby as the one her stepsister has on?'

Mia held her breath in horror, her hands tightening together in her lap. Would they find her here overhearing this? She swallowed and sat very still.

The other girl laughed. 'Never. The mother looks as if she has ambitions for her younger daughter and watches Mr Kevin Allan with an intent that is embarrassing, though I should imagine it will all come to nothing and Mr Allan will move on to a more suitable prospect before long. The family has neither money, class nor manners, unlike Mr Rushworth, who is blessed in an abundance of them all.'

The music seemed to have changed and, on hearing it the two young ladies rushed out to partake in whichever dance had now commenced, leaving Mia alone and wondering how safe it would be to show herself. The night and all its gaiety crashed down upon her and she understood with a dawning certainty how little her family was actually welcomed here. A beautiful sister who had turned the head of an eligible young nobleman, a mother who was desperate and showing it, and an older spinster sibling who looked like a drab in her outdated and unfashionable blue gown.

Unclasping her mother's necklace, she slipped it away in her pocket, desperate to hide such embellishment with a growing apprehension. This was why she seldom ventured into society. People here were not kind and any perception of attempting to gain more than your given due was slapped down perfunctorily.

They were outsiders with little in the way of funds to recommend them. What a woman might lack in looks and personality was quickly made up for in terms of fortune, title or land.

Having none of these things, Mia was glad suddenly that Susan and Lucille had been invited to Bath. Perhaps there they would thrive in a way that was impossible in London, her own presence amid the group patently unhelpful.

Leaving her sanctuary, she glanced at herself in a mirror, trying to find some protection in bravery. Her expression looked false and fraught, but there was nothing else for it. She could not stay secreted away all evening and she would not flee.

No, Susan deserved her chance at something and if even half the young ladies here thought the same way as those she had just overheard, then she needed to be by her sister's side. Protecting her.

As she wended her way through the room, Mia's eye was caught by a painting on a wall just to one side of the room and, intrigued, went across to look. It was a huge summer pastoral scene and for a moment she lost herself in the simple joy of it. Oh, to be there in the countryside surrounded by fields and trees and houses that looked as if they had withstood the test of time. To be sitting by that river and in the shade of those trees, far from anyone and everything.

'Good evening.'

She knew the voice before she turned, that deep rawness she remembered from the docks.

Up close and under the lights he was breathtaking, his eyes now lighter than she had thought them, dark brown with shards of caramel. When he did not continue speaking, she formulated a reply of her own, trying with all her heart to make her voice sound normal.

'It is good to see you here, sir, if only because I would like to thank you for your kind gesture the other afternoon. I hope the carriage returned to collect you post-haste and that you made your way from the port with ease.'

Stop talking, she thought, and swallowed with an effort.

'It did not matter after all, for we found another conveyance the moment the one you were in had left.'

'Then I am most relieved, for the day was very cold and on the way home we saw no other transport that might have been able to convey you to where you were going.'

More words than were needed. She resolved to say no more. The silence between them was growing and a certain awkwardness made her bite her lip.

'Are you here with your family?'

The question surprised her and in his eyes a wariness was growing.

'I am. Mama is here and also my sister, Susan.' Better. Not so verbose. A simple answer that was to the point.

'The dark-haired girl in the golden gown?'

His knowledge of her stepsister unsettled her and her nerves were back. 'Ah, you have seen her? She gives the impression she might be demanding, but she isn't really and I honestly feel that the suitor who finally persuades her to be his bride will be a lucky man.'

This time a smile crossed his face.

'Lucky, indeed.'

But his tone held no inkling of what his words implied, leaving her at a loss as to what to say next.

'I saw you slip from the room a few moments ago. I wondered where you had gone so I came looking.'

'You left the large group of people around you to find me?'

'They are all old friends.'

'And ones who no doubt were glad to see you back in England, given you have just returned from somewhere far away?'

'India.'

'India?'

'I trade in cloth and spices.'

'I smelt it on you at the docks.'

He frowned and, realising her misstep, Mia filled in the discomfort with words. 'I am Miss Euphemia

Denniston. My stepmother, stepsister and I reside in Bolton Street.'

'Euphemia? An unusual name.'

'It was my father's choice and because he had some affection for medieval Swedish literature he decided upon it...' She stopped, trying to moderate her effusiveness. 'My family calls me Mia.'

'A gentler version.'

His speech was always precise, clipped even, and he did not waste words, but there was something in the way he looked at her that was mesmerising, something that made her feel as if he saw beyond her tightly wound hair and the quality of her dress. Something dangerous and dark and exciting.

When music from the band started up she stayed still. A waltz. He would leave her now to dance with one of the beautiful young women surrounding him. Her breath caught and held as he put out his hand.

'Will you dance?'

'With you?' She heard the surprise in her words even as he nodded and then he was escorting her out on to the floor, through a crowd of people watching, the buzz of speculation growing by the second.

She had danced in public three times in all of her life, the only other waltz with the first Mr Rushworth just before he had whisked her out of the main salon and into ruin, and so when this new one placed one hand at her waist as the other clasped her fingers, she jumped in nervousness, an action that brought his glance directly to hers.

'I am somewhat unpractised, but I will attempt not to stand on your feet.'

The bracelet with the strange markings fell over his cuff, the silver catching the light from above. As they danced she saw Lucille and Susan looking on at them from one edge of the floor, mouths open with astonishment.

'Your stepmother looks very much recovered.'

'She is. It was the cold, I think, that made her unwell. She has never liked the winter very much, you see, and that day the Frost Fair was a freezing place to be and one she decided was not quite to her taste and—'

His hand tightened on hers.

'Miss Denniston?'

'Yes?'

'Do you always talk so much?'

For a second, shock kept her mute, but then a stronger instinct surfaced.

'I do, Mr Rushworth.' She lifted her chin to see what it was he might say next, but he laughed and let it go. She remembered this feeling in society as a seventeen-year-old, this feeling of never being good enough, of needing to change in order to suit others, and although she, too, was sometimes exasperated by her nervous ramblings, she was determined he would not know of it. 'I talk because I want you to know that my stepsister is a gentle young woman who is most adept at the art of managing a well-kept house.'

'And why should you see the need to tell me this?'

'I am telling you this because Susan is here in her

first Season, sir, and I would imagine you to be a good catch, so to speak.'

Mia knew she was being blunt, but couldn't help herself.

'A good catch?'

'For a young girl who has come here to find a husband. Confident. Rich. Kind, I hope?' She hated the blush that she could feel staining her cheeks. 'I do think you are that.'

'Are you always so honest, Miss Denniston?'

She pondered that. 'I used not to be.'

'What changed then?'

'Experience and circumstance, for it seems that life passes by those who are not bold.'

'Your life?'

'Pardon?'

'Are you speaking of your life or of your sister's?'

'My sister's. She is the one who is here to find a husband.'

'But you have not the inclination for a husband of your own?'

'Of course not. I am too old and too poor.'

'How old?'

'Almost thirty-one. Ancient.'

'You look younger.'

'I think, Mr Rushworth, that India may have affected your eyesight. Perhaps a pair of English spectacles may bring things more firmly into focus.'

He stopped at that, right in the middle of the dance floor, his hand still in hers, but his feet unmoving.

'Why are you not married, Miss Denniston? Why has your hand not been won?'

Now he was being blunt in his turn.

'Is this a joke, sir?' She tried to disengage his grip because his words were perplexing, but he would not let her go as they began to dance once again.

'My friends told me that they have not seen you at all in society. They say that you left it very abruptly years ago after a promising start and I am wondering why?'

He had discussed her with his friends? Mia could find no answer to his query and remained mute with terror, such a fine line between now and then. No one had ever asked these questions of her, not even her father, who had simply taken her word that she no longer desired to be out in society. Lionel Denniston had cancelled other arrangements and sold the few gowns that he had procured for her for almost the exact same price that he had paid for them.

And afterwards her services to the family had resumed in the same pattern as they had before. She helped manage the house and tallied up the family's growing bills, the money which had been her father's birthright having largely dwindled by the time she was twenty. Lucille Denniston had not insisted on any other understanding either, but had been well pleased with her help in all of the many duties a household required.

Augustus Rushworth was a man who looked as if nothing could rattle him, a man whose life had probably gone splendidly, a man of worth. Everything about him exuded wealth for his clothes were of the very best quality and the boots he wore looked new and shiny.

'I left society because there were other things that made more sense to me and that I enjoyed doing more. I am not an interesting woman, Mr Rushworth. I have little inclination for these sorts of events and have no interest at all in needlework or the pianoforte.'

'Do I look like a man who would require that?'

He surprised her with his question.

'No. You look like someone who would be more at home on a horse discovering new lands or in a war facing an enemy. I imagine your life has been a fascinating one, given the general reaction of people here in this room when you were first announced.'

For all the time they had spoken she had noticed people watching him.

'I am also supposing you are well heeled and well brought up. A man who would easily convince the girl he decided upon to become his wife.'

'Your suppositions have large gaps in them, Miss Denniston, for I am as little interested in the marriage mart as you proclaim yourself to be.'

She felt him shift her carefully to the side of the floor, the music running down to the end of the dance. A few more seconds and it would finish and she doubted she would ever see him again. She had been too forward and too honest, traits that were not valued here in society. Men wanted women they could mould, pliant and biddable companions who would not be demanding or difficult. Perhaps he thought such qualities would run in her family?

'I am sorry for my misguided assumptions, sir, and I thank you for the dance.' She got this in just before the final flourish of the orchestra and he bowed his head to her.

'It was my pleasure, Miss Euphemia Denniston.' Her name on his lips sounded fascinating in a way it never had before, though surely he had not intended it so.

Her stepmother pounced as soon as he let her go, pushing between them with intent in her eyes.

'It is so good to have this chance to thank you for your help the other day, Mr Rushworth. We had hoped to see you again to offer you our most sincere gratitude and, lo and behold, here is our chance...'

Lucille left the statement open.

He merely tipped his head, giving Mia the impression that he wished to be anywhere but here.

'Susan, my love,' Lucille then said, pulling her into notice. 'I would like to properly introduce my daughter to you, if I may, for it was such a brief encounter the other day.'

Susan looked more shy than Mia had ever seen her and the blush that covered her cheeks spoke volumes.

Her stepsister liked him. Suddenly everything took on another peril, one that Mia had not wholly recognised before. Susan's penchant for Mr Rushworth would be nothing short of a disaster, Mia's own foolish yearning from years back coming to mind. Why had she not seen that when she had praised her stepsister to him in the dance?

'It is so good to meet you, Mr Rushworth. So very good, indeed.' Susan sounded breathless and eager. She also sounded very young.

He smiled, but in a manner that did not look quite real. Certainly he smiled at her sister in a way far different to how he had smiled at her.

Lucille appeared thrilled and grateful. Could it get any worse? But when Susan spoke next, Mia had her answer: yes.

'You dance very well, sir,' said Susan, every word angling for her own invitation.

'You are very kind, Miss Denniston.' His voice seemed to come from a distance as Mia recognised something in him, the tip of his head, the way the light caught the cleft in his chin, the long, planed angle of his cheeks in the shadows cast by the light in the room. Beautiful. Familiar. She felt sick, her mind reaching for her counting method of breathing, but the world swirled on its point and then receded into a blackness that she had no hope of stopping.

Augustus caught Miss Denniston before she fell too far and lifted her into his arms. She weighed nothing at all, her head falling against his shoulder as he walked, her family behind them and all eyes turned to the spectacle.

What the hell had just happened? Was Euphemia Denniston unwell? Did she have some malady that made her susceptible to heat or had she taken one too many glasses of the wine on offer?

Bram Baker-Hill, seeing the consternation, had joined him, but Augustus wished they were alone. He wished everyone might leave him with Euphemia so that he could ask her properly about what had just occurred, for he had seen in her eyes some recognition that was puzzling. The Allans were here now, gesturing him in to a small salon to one side of the main room, and he made to follow.

He laid her down carefully on a sofa, plumping up a cushion to keep her from falling, and as she came to there was mortification on her face.

Without waiting, she struggled up, pushing the cushion away and sitting, smoothing her skirts down as she did so, her hands shaking as she took stock.

He thought she might burst into tears for a moment, but she didn't. Instead, she swallowed twice and tried to smile.

'I am so sorry. I don't know…what happened.'

'You fainted, Mia, and Mr Rushworth caught you and carried you in here.' These were her sister's words and Euphemia Denniston flinched, her fingers clenching at the sofa beneath her, grasping the fabric as if to keep herself steady.

'How do you feel now?' He kept his voice low.

'I am fine.'

She did not look at him, but glanced away at all the people who were in the room, their expressions full of curiosity.

A doctor then appeared, bag in hand, a competent-looking physician who demanded that the room be cleared.

'I want family only here while I examine my patient,' the man said in a voice that brooked no argument. Augustus made to stand, though at that second her hand reached out to him, her blue eyes holding a desperate sadness.

'It's all right,' he stated firmly because he could not work out quite what else to say.

'No,' she replied. 'It is not and it never will be.'

And then she looked away.

Outside the room, Bram placed an arm on his shoulder. 'What was that about?'

'I have no idea.'

He heard the gossip all around as he walked with Bramwell, the hearsay and the tittle-tattle. It was the way of the London salons just as surely as it was of the Indian courts. People enjoyed a mystery and Miss Euphemia Denniston was a veritable one. She was beautiful and she was hidden. That word surprised him, but it fitted her exactly. Her tightly bundled hair and the ancient dress. Her demeanour among society and her quiet smile. She was nothing like the other women here, with their designs and their expectations.

She didn't flirt. She stood away from others. When he had seen her from his place near the pillars he had been watching her for a good five minutes and she'd had a certain air of resignation, of fortitude and nervousness, that was at odds with a room full of gaiety and merriment.

She didn't want to be present, that was plain. She was not looking for a husband and did not relish being thrown into such a situation. It was the sister she was here for, to aid her chances in finding a good match, to chaperon and to protect.

Why hadn't Miss Euphemia Denniston married? Why had she had disappeared from society almost as soon as she had arrived in it all those years ago? Her hairstyle posed questions, too, pulled back as it was into a tight and unflattering knot, the colour dimmed by what appeared to be thickly applied oil that left it flat and lifeless.

It was as if she had looked carefully at herself in a mirror and decided on all the measures she could take to make herself appear plainer. The pearls which he had seen on her earlier in the evening had been removed and he wondered why she cloaked herself in dullness, rendering an invisibility that was intriguing. What would her hair look like set free in the wind? The wheat and gold he had glimpsed in it was intriguing.

When he had danced with her, he had felt curves that were not revealed in the shapeless dress she wore—a further camouflage that was confusing, for every other young woman in the room would have readily displayed such assets.

He tried to smile as Miss Annabelle Langham found him again and caught at his arm like a limpet. The implications of such an overt claim worried him, but he could do nothing save return to the circle of his friends, Miss Langham chattering on about 'poor old Miss Denniston who had an unusual name that no one could ever remember'.

Chapter Three

'Mr Rushworth danced with Miss Langham after you left, Mia, and then he danced with all the most beautiful girls in the room—including myself, I might add, though Mr Allan was most insistent that I partner him in the one waltz left so unfortunately it was only in a quadrille that I stood up with Augustus Rushworth.' She used his name in a familiar way and laughed. 'It is whispered that he was married in India in a city called Bombay which sits on the water.'

'Was?' Mia could not help but ask.

'I heard one woman say that he had lost her.'

'Lost her how?'

'I don't know. Mama started talking and I couldn't overhear any more. One thing I do know is that every woman in the room sought Mr Rushworth out, even the older ladies.'

'More of a reason to be wary of him, then, I should think.'

'Mama likes him.'

Mia's heart sank.

'She said that the bride who finally marries him will be a lucky woman indeed because his lands and houses are extensive and his wife would never have to worry about money again. Imagine that. To be able to buy exactly what you might desire and never fret about it.'

'There would be a price to pay, I fear, Susan.'

'Oh, you are such a killjoy sometimes, Euphemia. One is allowed dreams, after all, but perhaps your sourness is because you were so unwell last night so I should try to dredge up some sympathy. Are you feeling better this morning?'

'Much better.' She did not wish for further discussion of her unusual behaviour.

'I wonder when we might see Mr Rushworth next?'

That thought made Mia frown. She wouldn't see him again, she was sure of it, for her ridiculous faint had probably frightened off a man like that and her words had hardly been careful ones. She changed the subject.

'The young Mr Allan appeared to be most enamoured with you. He seems like a nice boy?'

'And that is the problem, Mia. He is a boy whereas Mr Rushworth is a man.' She ran a hand across her temples. 'But all this talk is giving me a headache and so I am going to take to my bed to try to chase it away. I will not rise until the evening and I shall dream of the fascinating Augustus Rushworth and you, my unhappy sister, will not be able to stop me.'

When Susan left, Euphemia threw a shawl around her shoulders on top of her nightgown and went to the blue gown hung in its bag of cloth by the wardrobe, pulling apart the material in the deep skirt pocket to locate her pearls.

They were not there.

She searched again in the same pocket and in the other one, her fingers flying over all the garment. Her mother's pearl necklace was missing.

Had it dropped out as Augustus Rushworth had carried her in to the side salon after she had fainted? Or had she lost it somewhere else? She shook her head hard, wondering how she might try to locate the pearls, and was furious at herself for taking them with her in the first place. It had been a vanity that had been rewarded by a loss. She had never once fainted in all of her life. Even after the awful incident in the street the day after the Dashwood ball, she had tidied herself up and carried on, endeavouring to forget and to allow no one else the knowledge of what had happened. Guilt had had its part, too, as had doubt and shame.

She would send a note to the Allans and enquire as to whether her necklace had been recovered somewhere in the room after the ball. Surely other people misplaced things at such occasions and it would not be considered in bad taste to ask?

'Mama. I wish I had known you.' She whispered the words, feeling that the last remaining link had been severed, a final breakage, an irretrievable forfeiture.

She would be thirty-one years old next week and, if she lost her place here in this house, she now had nothing of value left that she could pawn, should she need money. It was a warning and an omen. She had enjoyed dancing with Mr Rushworth too much. Women of her status should not be thinking such things, though, and her stepmother was probably already regretting her presence at the ball.

She had come home by herself, ushered into a hired hack and sent back to Bolton Street to allow Mama the much more important job of chaperoning Susan. The good fortune of meeting a man who was both wealthy and personable was not to be squandered, after all, and her stepsister's chance of a fine marriage lay in this Season only. An ageing spinster stepdaughter who had made a spectacle of herself could hardly be helpful and Mia knew she would need to impress upon her stepmother her most sincere apologies.

Walking over to a small set of drawers, she brought out her journal and jotted down a few of her thoughts from last night, making certain her notes were impersonal and careful, for Susan had a habit of reading the book and she did not want her sister to find anything that might incite comment.

Last night she had dreamed again and her lover had walked into the light with the unforgettable face of Mr Augustus Rushworth.

She'd recognised the likeness at the ball, too, just before she had fainted with the shock of it, and when he'd turned to leave her with the physician she had clutched at his hand, which had left him frowning.

Her stepmother had noticed her action, too, no doubt. She wanted to write about last night here in her diary, wanted to pour out words that might have helped her make sense of everything and instead...instead she had dreamed of him because it was safer.

Mr Rushworth made her feel safe, with his big, robust frame and a wide and well-inhabited life. He had lived in India and had married and lost a wife. He traded in spices and mysterious goods from the East and was the next male heir in line for the honour of the family title. A baron. Rich beyond measure with many friends and acquaintances.

He was a man who was well beyond her reach and would never settle for a wife who was not beautiful and accomplished and connected.

An original like Miss Annabelle Langham of the Asquith family. She was the kind of girl a titled and wealthy aristocrat married. Yet he had spoken to her and danced with her and lifted her up gently against him to make sure that she was safe.

'Euphemia.' Her name echoed in the corridor and her stepmother appeared. 'Are you going to get dressed and come and do the month's accounts? I have received a note from the butcher and doubt we can order any more meat until we pay him. Susan has retreated back to her bed for she has a headache and asks not to be disturbed until evening. I think it's a result of the excitement of her success last night, and success it truly was, no thanks at all to you.'

Scrambling up, Mia reached for her clothes, real life crashing in like a wave. Being busy was a buffer against excessive introspection. She could not change who she was and society was certainly not going to rearrange its expectations concerning beauty, eligibility or suitability.

The enigmatic Mr Rushworth would choose one of the originals of the Season and that would be that. She resolved that if she saw his face in her dreams tonight she would simply wish him gone, banished into the ether of unsuitability, for she could only be disappointed with such ridiculous hopes.

She was sensible, prudent and wise, all qualities that had allowed her a life worth living after she was attacked at the ball and then the next day on the street. She had no desire to conjure up another indiscretion and besides, after her ruin, she had never trusted her own reactions to any man. She blamed herself for the incidents, blamed her folly and her poor judgement.

Pulling on her third-best day dress and tying her hair in a simple ribbon of blue velvet, she found her stockings and shoes and went to join her stepmother.

The bell at the front door sounded a few hours later and Lucille bade her answer it as the kitchen lad had just been sent out to the markets and the other two housemaids were upstairs tidying away after the events of the previous evening.

Glad of the chance to stretch her legs after sitting at the figures for so long, Mia pulled the door open with a flourish to be met with the sight of Mr Rushworth dressed in his riding clothes and standing on their front step.

'You?'

The word was most discourteous, she knew, but shock had jolted away her manners and left her in speechless disbelief.

His gaze took in her dress and her hair and her very undone look, just as hers registered a snowy-white intricately tied cravat, a woollen jacket and trousers that must have cost a fortune, and boots of the finest leather she had ever seen, with her wavy reflection showing in the shine of their surface.

He doffed his hat and she noted that his hair today was loose again, curling at his nape, the darkest of blacks with a hint of deep brown.

'I hope you are feeling better today, Miss Denniston?'

'I am, thank you, Mr Rushworth.' Mia could not for the life of her work out why he was here, standing in her doorway at two-thirty in the afternoon of a cold and grey winter's day. She wrapped her arms across her chest, trying to hide even a little of her plain clothing, the blue ribbon that kept her hair tidy trailing down her front.

He appeared to wait for her to say more and, given that she always seemed to gabble so much in his company, she could hardly blame him for it. But she was out of words, out of breath and out of pride, the tired gown he had seen her in yesterday a thousand times more elegant than this one, which was shabby beyond repair.

With a sudden thought, she removed her patched apron and hung it on the peg behind her, seeing the house from his point of view as she did so—dark, cold and plain.

He must not come in, was her next thought, because the sitting salon on the ground floor was plainer again and the ledger that she had been working on held an accounting of their diminished finances. A man like him would take note of things, see the faded walls and the brighter spaces where pictures had been sold off to make ends meet. He would understand that the last chance this family had of survival was to have the twenty-year-old Susan married off to a man who might not find it onerous to help out the relatives.

'I am here, Miss Denniston, because I discovered your set of pearls pushed close against the wall beneath the landscape you had admired and I recognised them as the same set you were wearing earlier in the evening.'

He was holding them out to her now and Mia, hearing noises coming towards them, snatched at the necklace and pocketed it.

'They were my mother's.'

It was all she could say before Lucille descended upon them, her face lighting up when she saw Mr Rushworth, a visitor of such importance and distinction on her doorstep that it was unbelievable.

'Euphemia, why did you not say that Mr Rushworth had called upon us? Why have you left him standing here and not invited him in, for it is freezing outside? Unfortunately, Susan is still asleep, sir; the night's entertainment carried on very late, you see, though I can easily wake her—'

He interrupted her without compunction.

'I just came to make certain Miss Denniston was recovered. The Allans were most insistent that I ask after her and they furnished me with this address.'

'Euphemia?' The question in the word was pointed as her stepmother's eyes came around to her own. 'She is perfectly well this morning and embarrassed about the fuss she caused, no doubt. Her father, my late husband, was a man who suffered from frequent fainting fits, too, so perhaps it is some bothersome familial inheritance that weakens the blood. Susan, on the other hand, keeps unblemished health.'

Mia looked away from the brown eyes that now watched her and bit down on her reply. Lucille would not be pleased at Rushworth's concern, she knew that; the thought of an interest in anyone's well-being apart from her own daughter's was a distraction to her entire and sole focus which was to see Susan well married.

She almost wished her stepsister might come down the stairs at that moment, flushed from sleep and looking beautiful, and then all this hope could simply drain away to the place it belonged and her sister would be left to take her chances as she might. But Susan would not be up until at least the evening with the headache she complained of.

The clock in the hallway boomed out the three quarters of an hour, a whiny ring that had never sounded normal, and it was as if everything had conspired this morning to make Mr Rushworth scuttle away. The old dress, the pearls which she had not even had the time to thank him for properly and her stepmother's desperation to keep him here until Susan woke.

The rain was coming down harder, too, wetting the back of his jacket where the portico guttering had broken and was splashing his boots.

As if recognising the adversity of the weather, he tipped his head and made his farewell, jamming on his hat as he turned and made for his carriage, a footman jumping from the box seat to open the door for him.

Then the conveyance was gone, through the grey and the rain, swallowed up by gloom, the growing wind making their skirts move as they watched.

'Well, I never,' her stepmother said as she closed the door and went back into the sitting room. 'If I had not seen Mr Rushworth here on our doorstep with my own eyes I would never have believed it. What were you thinking not to ask him in immediately, Euphemia? What must he think of your manners? And why was Susan not here to receive him as she should have been? It was surely her he was after and to have missed such a wonderful chance...'

Lucille hurried away up the staircase to the bedrooms on the next floor, calling her daughter's name in a loud and insistent tone, the very disbelief of having received such a gentleman evident in every single shrieked word.

Stunned by what had happened, Mia just stood there, her hand in the pocket with the pearls, wrapped around the warmth he had imbued into them, astonished by his gesture.

He had brought them to her himself. He had not handed them to the host of the ball or ignored them altogether, the chore of delivering lost jewellery in a rainstorm far beneath the calling for a man of his rank.

Why?

He had not stayed to wait for her sister or taken up the opportunity to come inside to the warmth. He hadn't looked pleased, either, as he'd handed her the necklace, a solemn man with much on his mind.

She would send him a note, she resolved, to make up for her lack of manners in thanking him. She would say that the pearls were precious to her and she would not have wanted to lose them. He was staying at the Rushworth town house in St James's Square; she had heard the woman standing next to her mention it at the ball when Mr Rushworth had first been announced.

The lost heir, rich beyond measure and wild in his youth.

As wild as his brother? The thought was disconcerting, but then he did that to her—tipped her balance and made her believe in things that would never come to pass.

Women of her age and station should not have such delusions.

She wished she had someone to confide in and talk with, someone she could ask for advice, but friends had been hard to find in a life that demanded all her energy to simply survive.

A shout from upstairs told her that her stepsister had just been informed of their unexpected visitor and she wondered what Lucille had said to Susan to explain his presence at their doorstep.

Probably she had urged excitement and hope, all the usual and ordinary suitors set aside for the possibility of this one remarkable and miraculous newcomer. Her sister would be thrilled as well, no doubt, and any plans to go to Bath were probably going to be put off. They had their rainbow with the pot of gold here, unmarried, newly arrived back in England, his estates calling for a marriage with heirs to bind the future.

Mia shook her head and dragged out her pearls, thankful for their return and confused at the same time.

When he had handed them over she had felt his fingers touch hers, a momentary and fleeting connection before she had snatched hers away. Had she imagined it? She was certain she must have and that in itself brought up other new and more worrying questions.

Augustus watched the streets of London pass by from his side of the carriage window.

That meeting had not gone as he had planned at all. He had hoped he might get a few moments alone with Miss Denniston as he gave her the pearls, but instead...

He leaned back against the cushioned seat and thought of the strange encounter. She'd seemed scared and as she had snatched the pearls away from him his fingers had curled around hers in an instinctive reflex, to keep her safe, to keep her close. There was no reason for him to have done so and he had seen the shock of the touch in her eyes before her stepmother had come to join her.

Euphemia Denniston was prone to fits of fainting like her father, by the sounds of it, and even standing at her own doorway she had appeared nervous and uncertain. Well, he had his answer on one thing at least. Her hair this morning had been golden and wheat-coloured, fluffing into curls around her face and reaching down to the middle of her back, the blue velvet ribbon loosely tied around the thickness.

He smiled at this recollection even as he mulled over the effect she was having on him. Her stepmother had thought he was there to see the younger daughter, by all accounts, and he thanked God the girl had still been asleep in bed. He had danced with her once last night and although she was nearly as beautiful as her sister but in a darker fashion, she was also young and silly.

He did not need another young and silly bride.

Augustus wished he could have gone back again, but he could not be certain what his reception might be, for when his fingers had tightened on hers all he had felt was the struggle to escape.

He closed his eyes and thought. He had married Jane Watson on a whim and regretted it. Was there some sort of fatal pattern in his attraction to women, a trait that kept recurring generation after generation? His grandfather, his father and his brother, and now him.

Euphemia Denniston was unusual and prickly and she had done little to encourage him to believe she might enjoy his company. Their one dance had been quickly over, her chatter showing only nerves, and yet holding her against him in a room full of people had seemed…right.

Opening his eyes, he shook his head. He was losing his mind perhaps, given all that had happened in the last few years; grief had a certain ability to alter sanity.

He would be expected to marry again and provide an heir—his grandfather had already dispatched a letter to him in India which set out as much—and as the last hope of the lineage of the Rushworths he understood the responsibility. He had seen it first-hand in the Allans' ballroom with the crush of suitable candidates lining up in front of him all night, the expectation of a possible betrothal written plainly.

But a face with freckles, dimples and a worn timidity came to mind and he shook it away. Duty was a harsh calling, but given the path his life had taken he needed to answer the summons. There were sins he had to pay for and he could no longer ignore them. But not yet. He needed some time and space to simply be, to enjoy what England had to offer without shackles tying him down.

He would build in the countryside. He would find some land and construct a house. Ten years in the proximity of the overcrowded and busy Bombay had given him a love of peace. He needed to find a quietness that had long been denied to him, but first he needed to see his grandfather to bid for some solitude.

He'd heard the name of the Bambury daughter yesterday evening in the salons of the Allans' town house. He'd been promised in marriage to Miss Felicity Bambury by his father when he was young, a sort of practical alliance between two landowning families with shared borders in Cheshire. When he'd left England quickly and married almost as fast in India, he had expected such a troth to have been made null and void. But it seemed the Bambury girl was still not betrothed and he hoped these earlier promises would not now cause a problem.

In truth he thought he would never marry again as his heart had been torn apart so forcibly by the death of his daughter he was sure that the broken pieces left would have no chance of reforming into something usable. That was the reason he had been so surprised by his reactions to Miss Euphemia Denniston. He wanted to keep her safe from the sadness he could see in her eyes because it was the same defeat of hope he could see in his own sometimes. She was a kindred spirit, the complexity of loss marking her just as it had done him.

Euphemia met Mr Rushworth in the park the next afternoon on a pathway that was more usually empty and one she often used. At her age she was not forced to take a maid with her at every small outing and they hadn't the number of servants to accommodate such a want anyway.

He was standing still and watching her and she had no option but to keep walking and meet him, her heart thumping with the unexpectedness of it.

'Do you come here often, Miss Denniston?'

'Nearly every day, Mr Rushworth. It is a quiet pathway.'

'Which is why I chose it, too.'

Mia frowned. Did he mean he preferred his own company by those words? Should she then walk by and leave him to his solitary thoughts?

No. The opportunity of this meeting was not one she could squander. 'I was going to send you a note to say a proper thank you for the return of my pearls. I told you they were my mother's, but what I did not tell you was that they are the only thing I have left of her and so they are very precious to me.'

'When did your mother die?'

'When I was born.'

'Mine did, too.'

He looked as though he wanted to swallow these words as soon as he had said them and she felt a sadness well up into her throat, one so forcible she could not speak. He would know what losing a mother was like. He would understand the grief as few others would. It was a connection that was poignant.

'I did not know her at all,' she continued, because for the first time in all her life she wanted to tell someone what she felt. 'My father never spoke of her again.'

'You might have been luckier than me, then. My father spoke of my mother so much it sent him mad and none of it was flattering.'

Astonishment kept her quiet.

'The marriages of the Rushworths down through the centuries have been miserable affairs. Surely you have heard the rampant gossip of such a curse?'

She shook her head. 'I am not out and about in society much, sir, and when I am no one really speaks to me.'

He laughed.

'I like your honesty.'

'It is one of the many faults my stepmother keeps telling me I have.'

'Why would she do that?'

'Irritation, I suppose. It cannot be easy to be stuck with the daughter of a husband whom she was not much enamoured with at the end.'

Her reply surprised her for she rarely spoke to anyone at length outside her family. But she was tired of all the lies and it did not seem quite right to be untruthful to a man whose face inhabited her nightly dreams.

'Would you allow me to escort you to the Barretts' ball next Monday, Miss Denniston?'

Shock hit her. Was he saying what she thought he was, and why on earth would it be she he was asking?

'I am not sure you understand how much of a social pariah I am, Mr Rushworth. I would not be a wise choice if you need to regain a social standing here...'

He stopped her.

'But I don't.'

'In fact, people might wonder why you were desperate enough to ask me.'

'We will let them wonder.'

If his own status did not bother him, then she would need to take another tack. 'I'd have nothing to wear...'

'I will send you a gown.'

The jolt of such words astounded her. 'You cannot,

sir! It would be a scandal if you did so and one I would not welcome. There is no way in the world that I could say yes to such a suggestion.'

'No one needs to know I purchased the dress.'

'My stepmother and stepsister would hardly miss such a thing.'

'They are off to Bath, I have heard. Your stepsister told me of it herself. She also said that you were not invited. Perhaps you should use this opportunity to take a risk and live.'

That angered her. 'You think I don't. You know nothing of me, sir.'

'I know you hide things. I know you are not ancient, although you pretend it. I know you secrete yourself away behind large plants at a ball to gather some relief from the constant pressure of people. I know you fainted the other evening, although I doubt you do that easily, despite what your stepmother says, for you seem a lot stronger than she might allow.'

Swallowing, Mia looked away, staggered by his words.

'The truth is, Miss Denniston, that I do not wish to be married right away. You told me you did not desire to be, either. We could help each other. I am besieged by debutantes and their desperate mothers everywhere I go and the thought came to me last night that perhaps you could protect me from them.'

This conversation was becoming so ridiculous that Mia began to laugh.

'Protect you? Mice do not protect lions, Mr Rushworth.'

'Allow me the chance to show you that they do, for you would look incomparable in gold satin.'

Augustus knew the moment he gave the compliment that it had been the wrong thing to say. He saw her close up like a flower without the light, tensed into leaving, a frown across her forehead that had not been there a second ago.

'Just a chance, Miss Denniston. Only that.'

He brought things back to the formal, scrambling for reason, although in truth there was no logic in what he was offering.

'I would like to escort you to some events across the next month. This would please my grandfather, who is adamant I am seen out in society. It would also allow me the time to find a place in the country to which I may disappear, somewhere quiet. I should not expect you to be anything you did not wish to be. All I need is your arm across mine so that young women of the likes of Miss Annabelle Langham do not see me as a marriage prospect and subsequently leave me alone. Just for a month.'

'I am not a woman who could pretend...'

'And I don't want you to be. I want a companion, someone who thinks about marriage along the same lines as I do.'

'No one would believe you have chosen me.'

'I believe you sell yourself short and have done so for so long now that you think it true.'

A sky-blue glance raked across his, fiery in denial.

'And your friends? What would they make of such a scheme?'

'I would not tell them all of it. It is between you and me. No one else needs to know.'

She was biting at her bottom lip now and the dimples of perplexity were fully on show.

'Why is it you are offering this chance to me, Mr Rushworth? A hundred other women would jump at such a proposition and without subterfuge or prompting.'

'But that is the difference, Miss Denniston. As I have stated, with other women such a charade could end up in exactly the place that I do not wish to be.'

'Married?'

'Precisely. If it is a slight inducement, I might add that your own reputation would be enhanced by our association.'

He saw the fury even before she looked away.

'I am not concerned about my reputation, sir. I do not have any desire to conform to the expectations of society and if you think I do then you are even more mistaken than I had imagined.'

'I offer this only out of the hope that such an idea might be helpful to us both, Euphemia. If you want to cling to me all night so as to avoid conversation with others, I would welcome it. Our agreement would simply be a mutual desire to avoid the expectations of others and as soon as you decide you no longer wish to participate you would simply need to tell me.'

'And that would be the end?'

'I promise it.' He placed his right hand over his heart and saw her looking at the silver bangle around his wrist.

'What did you do in India, Mr Rushworth?'

'I was one of the principals for the East India Company. I traded in spices and cloth, as I told you, but I was also an envoy for the King.'

'An envoy?'

'An intermediary between the Crown and the Indian states.'

'No wonder you are persuasive then in your arguments. Did you inveigle the leaders there to do exactly as you bade them?'

'Not always. There was some leeway in the authority of the Crown and they understood that, but I travelled a lot and spoke their languages so I suppose most of them trusted me, knew me...' He trailed off because there had been times when trust had been broken by others and he'd had no power to change it. It was another of the reasons why he had returned home, the unending greed of the East India Company sickening him.

'The other night at the ball I heard someone say that you married there. I also heard that you had lost her?'

Surprise kept him still. 'My wife died from cholera two years ago.'

'Did you get sick as well?'

'No, I was away in Ceylon at the time. It is an island sitting to the south in the Bay of Bengal. Jane, my wife, had had visitors from Calcutta in the west and it was believed that they were the carriers for there had been a small outbreak in the area in which they lived.' He tried to keep the vitriol from his voice as he gave her this explanation.

'That must have been a hard thing for you to be so far away while she was sick.'

He nodded, thinking only of Alice. Euphemia did not ask any more, but looked across to the river, various emotions running over her face. Augustus thought she had never looked more beautiful.

'If my stepmother and stepsister do go to Bath, then your suggestion might be manageable, Mr Rushworth, but please do not send the dress to me until after they have departed, and I shan't keep it. It will merely be on loan for our...agreement.'

'Very well.'

He couldn't believe she was going to say yes.

She was small and brave, the upturned collar of her cloak showing up her paleness. She was unlike any other woman he had ever encountered and one divorced from all the deceit of society. There was an honesty in her that was a relief after years of trying to determine the motives of others, the natural comeliness he had seen that first second of meeting her on the docks in the frost even more astonishing now. He imagined her in a gown that was not ill fitted, one that brought out the colour of her skin and the gold in her hair.

Euphemia Denniston had declared that no one would

believe he had chosen her, but Augustus was certain once they saw her no one would believe otherwise.

He hoped this pact of theirs might be helpful to them both. On his part he simply needed a break from the pressure of being the heir to the title and the owner of a fortune. He needed some peace and quiet and the space to reintegrate into society here before he decided the shape of his future. If Miss Denniston could help him do that, he would be eternally grateful.

Without meaning to, he reached over and took her hand in his, liking the littleness, liking the warmth. He knew there were things she was not telling him, things that had made her the woman she now was, withdrawn from society and hiding her good looks.

'I promise you truth, Euphemia, in anything you ask of me, but I wonder if I could elicit the same from you? I don't want…complications or difficulties…'

'Difficulties?'

'Each of us has a history behind us, in which dwell secrets no doubt, but I am asking you for a commitment to the honesty of our unusual agreement and the pledge that if you do find a problem you will approach me with it first.'

'To solve?' She smiled at that and the display of her humour distracted him.

'In India my job was to do just that and I was good at it.'

'I have no doubt you were, Mr Rushworth.'

Augustus had the strange sensation that she was teasing him gently, the timid, nervous Miss Denniston revealing that beneath the surface there lay a woman who was much less likely to do as was expected.

'Perhaps you could make it known to your step-mother that I have intentions of removing myself immediately to Bath for a week or so?'

'My sister will be disappointed to find that not to be the case, sir, when she arrives there.'

'I think we both know that she needs a boy like the young Mr Allan to make her happy.'

His hand tightened on hers.

'I think we also know that the value of her youth would be lost on me.'

'You are not seeking a younger bride then, Mr Rush-worth?'

'Decidedly not. I am twenty-nine years old and too jaded and cynical to look for such innocence in others.'

Euphemia pulled her hand away; this conversation was getting more and more unusual. She wondered how old his wife had been, but did not feel up to asking, for her head was still spinning with all that they had discussed. He was younger than her by nearly two years and those years all of a sudden weighed her down.

He wanted her as a confidante...a friend, perhaps? A woman who would not expect things that he did not want to give. A pledge that had its limits and one with a clause to end it already built in. She mustn't read more into it.

She was hardly a beauty and this was a convenient arrangement with an expedient plan that gave no authority to feelings. But it was also one that could actually suit her. For him the benefit lay in being less available, but for her it lay in being more so. She had strayed too far from life for years and this was her last chance of ever righting the balance, a chance of social conviviality and an escape from the extreme loneliness that had been her closest companion ever since the Dashwood ball all those years ago.

A chance not of marriage or love, but at least of friendship. She felt comfortable talking with Augustus Rushworth and quietly offering her opinions. She was no longer overcome with too many words or struck down by a deathly silence. He encouraged her ideas, if truth be known, and looked at her as if she were... valuable to him. Valuable in a way she had never been to anyone before.

'I hope the gown you choose for me is...modest, sir. I should not feel comfortable in one that was not.'

'Modest like the navy blue dress you wore at the Allans'?' There was a lilt in his words that made her frown. 'The one that would not have been out of place at a Quaker meeting.'

'Well, the Quakers do say that plain dress, plain speech and piety are a battleground against vanity.'

He laughed. 'I see you know of their ways. You are not, by chance, one of them, are you?'

'A Quaker? No, but I read a lot. That way even when you are not in the world the world can still be a part of you.'

'Where do you get your books?' He appeared genuinely interested.

'Lackington, Allen & Co. at Finsbury Square. I have a subscription allowing me twelve books a year and their catalogue is most impressive.'

'There is a generous library at the Rushworth town house if you wish to peruse that. My great-grandmother left provision in a will to have it newly stocked each year as a sort of insult to her nearly illiterate husband.'

'One of the disastrous Rushworth marriages that you spoke of before?'

'Not quite. My great-grandmother managed to live with my great-grandfather for all the years of her life, if not in marital bliss, then certainly in civility, so I suppose their union was one of the most successful in recent times. When she died, he had the image of a pile of books engraved on her tombstone and then decided to attempt reading some of those volumes that she had accrued.'

'Do you read, sir?'

'Hardly ever. In India I was too busy and before I left England I spent more time living life than reading about it.'

His words cut so close to her former thoughts that Mia blushed. If he saw the creeping stain of redness across her cheeks, he gave no comment.

'I would be interested to know what some of your favourite stories from Lackington's are, though?'

'History books. Books about other lands. Books on myths and legends. Novels of any kind. I like Henry

Fielding and Fanny Burney and Daniel Defoe and Richardson's *Clarissa*—'

He interrupted her.

'The lady of the loveless marriage and an unending quest for virtue?'

'You think her wrong in that?'

'I think if I had been her I'd have been less insistent on everyone knowing my thoughts and just survived.'

'A quieter integrity, then?'

'Or none at all.'

She looked up at that and saw a darkness in his eyes and a lingering sadness, too. He was no longer thinking of books but of life, his life, and she wondered what had sent him to India in the first place when he was so young, and what had kept him there for a decade. She wondered at the scars on his hand, too, and the danger that was not quite hidden in every line of his body.

Yet he was kind to her and his conversation interesting and different.

'When you come with me to the Barretts' ball, will you wear your mother's pearls again, Euphemia? They suit you.'

She nodded because she could not find words to reply to the compliment and because for the first time since he had asked to escort her she could actually picture herself there.

'I will come and collect you at nine o'clock on Monday in my carriage. Is that suitable?'

'It is, sir.'

'Euphemia?'

'Yes.'

'Call me August.'

'Like a friend?'

'Indeed.'

He tipped his head at that and, looking around, Mia saw that the parkways had filled up with people striding here and there, many with glances directed their way.

She'd forgotten somehow that he was so known, so sought after, so very different from anything she was. She hoped that gossip of her standing alone with him in the park would not percolate down to her stepmother or stepsister.

Twelve days of freedom in front of her and a proposal that was making her heart beat faster. She would go with him to the ball because if she didn't she knew she would regret it for ever.

She watched him leave, striding across the green towards the roadway, every eye following him. She watched him until he was completely out of sight. The wind on her face smelt of winter and of freedom.

Chapter Four

His grandfather arrived at the Rushworth town house at three o'clock in the afternoon, just as his note had stated. He was a tall willowy man who'd aged only slightly in the ten years since Augustus had last seen him.

The butler showed him into the salon behind the dining room, a chamber enjoyed for both its warmth and its view. August had already instructed a servant to put out brandy and glasses.

'Rushworth.' The voice came from memory, softer now, less certain. 'I decided to come here to you as you did not seem willing to come to me.'

'I have been busy.'

'The busyness of a man who finds any excuse not to arrive where he should?'

'I am no longer nineteen, my lord. Your words have lost their power to hurt me and I owe you nothing.'

'Think you that you do not? Ah, indeed the title is entailed, but there is much in the way of the Rushworth wealth that is not.'

'Then give it away. Give it to anyone who might say exactly as you wish them to and be done with it.'

'You remind me of your mother.'

'Better than my father at least. Or my brother.'

'Alexandra was contrary and belligerent as well. She was also honest.'

'I'll take that as a compliment. What do you want?'

'I want you to return with me to Amerleigh House. I want you to see the estate as a man and not as a boy, for you must understand its place in history.'

'The history of our family?'

'No, the history of England. The fullness of time diminishes pettiness. I want you to see that.'

'You think my brother's actions petty?' Now true anger surfaced.

'I do not. I think you had full right to try and kill him and I damn well wish you had. I also wish my son had not taken Jeremy's side.'

'Hell.' This was unexpected. Augustus took a breath and poured himself a drink, watching as his grandfather did the same.

'But I was a parent and one day, when you become one, too, you might better understand the blinding need to protect your particular offspring. Against anything and anyone.'

That hit him in the gut. Alice. He finished the glass and poured another, feeling grief twist his heart and thicken his throat.

'You thought my father needed protecting? From what?'

'From himself. If his elder son was the full embodiment of a man with the devil inside him, then Vincent was not so far behind. I wanted it hidden, this fatal flaw of the Rushworths.'

'The flaw of jealousy?'

'No, anger. Unstoppable and unprovoked. They both made an art of it, though your brother had an edge that was far sharper. When he died I breathed a sigh of relief.'

His grandfather's eyes were now on him. 'Your hand is still scarred. They never disappeared?'

'If Jeremy was good at anything, it was maiming people with malice and elegance. I thought you understood that?'

'I did. It was why I sent Theodore Furlong with you to India.'

That news took Augustus aback. 'He never said that you did.'

'I asked him not to. He sent quarterly reports, though, to let me know exactly how you were faring. It seemed you did well, though his death a few years back meant I received no more word about you.'

Augustus ignored that because he did not want to know what detail had been in such letters. He needed no pity from a grandfather who had tossed him aside at nineteen, his hand and arm in tatters, blood dripping on the polished floorboards at Amerleigh House, his father screaming at him and using words that would never be forgotten.

'Why are you here?' With an effort he pulled himself back to the present.

'To ask you to come home.'

'Home?' He almost spat out the word. 'It is no longer that to me and never will be. I shall build elsewhere. Somewhere that is only mine.'

'Look at the estate first, Augustus. See it the way you were supposed to all those years before.'

'Before you betrayed me?'

'Before I got you out of harm's way.'

'The semantics of the guilty in the hope of atonement...'

'Which is all that is left to me.'

Augustus had had enough and stood.

'If I come, I will send word.'

A quick nod as his grandfather set the glass down on the table near him and then his relative was gone, the cold air from outside the house blowing in as he left, like a warning.

Relax and they will have you back exactly where they want you, he thought. *Give them an inch and they will want a mile.*

He wished Euphemia Denniston were here to talk to, to see his side of things, to understand that when it came to family there was never only black and white, and that the grey parts that ate at sense were also filled with sorrow and regret, just as much as they ever were with fury.

He remembered that cold November afternoon at Amerleigh House, the snow and the ice and the dark green pines, a sword in his hand as he battled for his life and lost his innocence.

Like Clarissa from the Richardson book. By the hand of others who should have wanted to keep him safe, but hadn't.

He'd been sick for three months, barely clinging to life as infection and fever burned through him, but Theo Furlong had done as his grandfather had asked and watched over him, refusing to allow the ease of death.

When he'd arrived in India he'd promptly married a girl who had given him her soft words and ripe body, and regretted it sorely before the next month was up.

Amerleigh House, the estate of divided loyalties and unmitigated treachery, and Bombay, the city where he knew finally that he could never escape the consequences of what had happened there.

They had finally left, her stepmother and sister, with trunks of clothes and all the trinkets needed for twelve days in Bath.

Husband hunting.

She had heard the name of Mr Rushworth so many times she felt faintly sick. They believed Augustus Rushworth would be in Bath because she had told them she had heard it said.

She wished the young and ardent Mr Allan might have arrived at their doorstep and demanded an audience to set things right because she was inclined to agree with Augustus Rushworth. Her stepsister needed a boy and not a man, a boy she could boss around and coddle and understand. Rushworth would eat Susan up in one small bite and he would never love her.

So in that way she had, after all, done her family a favour and saved them from the grief of an unsuitable alliance. She told herself that as she watched them go, the carriage of her stepmother's friend pulled by four fast and fine horses and her stepsister's gay waves all the way to the corner of the street.

Three days until the Barretts' ball. Seventy-two hours. Thousands of minutes. She was glad Lucille had taken the two best maids with them, leaving her with the young kitchen lad who skived off as often as he could and an elderly cook who was partially deaf and could not manage the stairs.

They were the bottom of the barrel as far as the calibre of help went, but she wouldn't be bothered by them. She could do as she wanted. The very thought of such liberty was exhilarating.

In the mid-afternoon there was a knock on the door and on opening it she saw that two liveried servants stood there, holding a set of large and carefully wrapped packages that she knew held the promised gown.

'Mr Rushworth asked that we deliver these parcels, Miss Denniston, and that we wait on your reply.'

The first man handed her a letter which she opened immediately.

I hope all is in order with this dispatch. Please do not hesitate to send me word if there are problems.

A lady's maid will arrive at your house on
Monday the eleventh at noon to help you dress
and I shall come to pick you up in my carriage
at nine o'clock.
Yours, etc.,
Rushworth

A formal letter. Just details. She wished there might have been something personal in it so she could deduce his state of mind. Was he regretting his proposal already? Had he rethought his plans and decided that even for him they were too scandalous, but felt that he should at least go through with this one event?

Her stepmother had friends in society, after all, so how long would it take for Lucille to hear the news from the Barretts' ball? A few days at most? And with a disgruntled would-be bride in tow? So many things she had not thought of when she had given her answer.

Yet she could not help but to have a peep under the wrappings.

The gold satin had a neckline that was nothing like she usually wore and he had taken no notice at all of her given preferences. This gown was low-cut and most daring. She could imagine very little of her chest would be left to the imagination once she had it on.

It was beautiful, though, with its elegant lines and pearl embellishments. The accompanying shoes were of white kid leather and the cloak was of a thick navy wool, any fussy detail lost in the quest for warmth.

The whole ensemble must have cost a fortune.

She asked the Rushworth servants to leave the packages in the side salon and showed them out after writing a quick note. Then she gathered her new belongings and walked up the stairs to her own room, locking the door behind her and leaning against it.

She was going to a ball and she felt like Cinderella of the fairy tale must have, her old blue gown replaced with a dress that seemed as if it was made of stardust and had just arrived from a fantasy. Lord Rushworth had turned into her unlikely fairy godmother, though none of these gifts would revert into something less at the strike of twelve.

Would the gown fit?

Unbuttoning her day dress, she peeled it off and, after removing her old and patched petticoat, felt the satin against her skin, pooling around her legs. The gold glowed in the daylight so she could only imagine what it might do at night-time. It fitted like a glove, the slip beneath decorated at the hem with rich lace and headed with a pearl trimming. The short Russian robe over-top was of the same fabric with laurel leaves embroidered at intervals with a similar sort of pearl. The neckline was low, the waist high and gathered, and the sleeves showed off smaller bands of pearls from top to bottom.

It was beautiful, the muted colour enhancing the gold in her hair and showing up the paleness of her skin.

She hardly looked like herself; she was a stranger bedecked suddenly in finery whereas before she had only known the second-hand, the old and the weary.

No one would believe it was she in this. No one

would comment on the shabbily dressed spinster sister behind her back, a snigger of pity inherent in every word.

She tried to pull the fabric of the bodice up a little but could not, her eyes taking in the visible swell of her breasts. Was the gown too showy, was her chest too bare? It was nowhere near as low as the horrible green gown her father had purchased, but still…

Crossing to the drawer beside her bed, she took out her mother's pearls and fastened them around her neck. Augustus Rushworth certainly had an eye for what jewellery might match this dress because the opaque gleam of the pearl necklace was reflected in the gold.

It was a miracle to have such clothes, here in her room, beautiful and completely suitable. Granted, her original introduction into society had meant a few gowns of better quality, but none of this standard, none studded in jewels or fitting with such exactitude.

Her father had purchased her coming-out dresses without any joy at all, the fewer coins needing to be spent the better, and when her Season had been deemed a failure very early on, he had sold them off while berating her for the bother of the purchase in the first place.

Euphemia hoped she was worth such largesse now and that after this one ball Rushworth would not think her as poor a bargain as her father had.

Her stepmother also worried her. The relationship between her and Lucille, while civil, had never been particularly warm and it would not take much for the perceived ties of responsibility to fray and snap. Did the

promise she had given to Augustus Rushworth consti-
tute a betrayal that would not be forgiven? What would
the consequences be should that be the case? Would she
be thrown from the house and into penury?

The world was not a safe place for her with its lack
of loyalty and questionable expectations. She had survived so far by keeping her head down and working
every hour of the day to remain a valuable member of
the household. But this…this gown could negate all of
that, for it would place her in a position where she was
no longer hidden and expose her to a society that in her
personal experience was seldom kind.

Should she cry off before more damage was done?
Should she send word to her stepmother about the fact
that Mr Augustus Rushworth was in London still and
that they should return post-haste? She stroked the
golden satin beneath her fingers, enjoying the finery
of the fabric and the beauty of its bejewelled embellishments.

Something in her understood that this would be her
very last chance to be a different woman and to rise
above all the misfortune that had come her way since
the moment she was born.

She would go to the ball wearing the dress Mr Rushworth had sent her and she would enjoy it. For once.
Without thinking of others or imagining terrifying consequences. The consequences of her choices thus far had
been brutally real and a small slice of pleasure would
not go amiss. She even went as far as to think she deserved some luck.

Mr Rushworth was neither ordinary nor insignificant, but then neither would he stay with her for long; their pledge was a temporary thing while he found his feet here in England and his place in the peace of the English countryside. After that she would have served her purpose as a shield and a ploy, and he would go back to the life to which he had been born: a future lord and next in line to the barony and all of the various estates entailed with the title.

He would need heirs and she would be thirty-one in two days, the years of her life fast running down into middle age. No, the chance of a fairy-tale night in a golden dress and pearls was too good an opportunity to miss simply because of fear. She would swallow up her misgivings and enjoy it—she was determined that she would.

There could never be any long-term arrangement between her and Augustus Rushworth because of her history with his brother. She could not live a lie of a life and she would never tell him what had happened to her, for just the thought of relating such a history to him made her feel sick.

She would take this offer in the spirit with which it had been offered and enjoy it, then he would move on and so would she. It was all she could hope for and all that she wanted.

The small voice inside her wished she were younger by a few years, younger than him at least and able to give him the needed heirs. But that was a foolish thought and she banished it as quickly as it had come.

* * *

He came to her at midnight, in silence. He took her hand and kissed it as he had done a hundred times before, softly and without expectation. She liked that about him, this reticence, this understanding, for she could pull away if she wanted and he would not insist on more.

She allowed him closer, stepping forward and feeling his body against her own, bound by moonlight and by shadow. He had grown taller, she thought, for the top of her head fitted beneath his chin now, tucked in together so that it was harder to move.

She frowned because this difference worried her. For so long now he had been exactly the same height as her and far less masculine.

She could not control this one, could not understand the needs she saw on his face, his eyes devouring her, his hands lifting.

She banished him with barely a thought, because if she did not know what he would do next then she did not want him here, unwieldy and unchecked...

Sitting up, Mia was jerked abruptly from her dream. She had seen parts of Rushworth in her dream man ever since she had met him at the dock, but now he seemed to have become wholly Rushworth—large, dangerous and no longer able to be manipulated.

The scene in the corridor with Augustus Rushworth's brother had left her fearful for years and with a frozen horror of anything physical. Her dreams were the last part of her that had allowed some release, but now...

He was not his brother, she knew that, of course, but her anxiety over time had not lessened the hurt of it somehow, leaving her stranded in a place that was impossible to move away from.

She was damaged from solitude and from isolation. She'd never had anyone to truly talk with or confide in and, although she was full of words, none of them meant anything. Susan laughed at her often about it, chastising her for her verbosity, her stepsister's demeanour so far from her own that Mia had no way of navigating a pathway to a shared understanding. Lucille mostly ignored her unless she needed something.

Mia had existed in a vacuum of fear and vulnerability, her father's lack of love only adding to the equation. Yet now she saw for the first time the chance of hope.

Hope that she could find a balance and a new normal, hope that she might rejoin a society she had left so many years ago, hope she would be happier and less...odd.

That thought made her frown. Augustus Rushworth would not wish to be saddled with an odd companion no matter how much she helped him. She would need to be less jagged and more calm, for all her fears were neither attractive nor common. She would need to be composed and serene, a woman who smiled more and talked less.

She could not expect universal acceptance but if even a few people began to like her she might manage.

If she could hold her head up and smile, she might be all right and in her golden gown she would not seem quite so much the ugly duckling she had always been.

Such a thing was possible and within days she would know if she had succeeded. 'Please God, help me,' she whispered into the night, the wind outside rising and the rain beating against the roof.

She was so glad her stepmother and stepsister had gone to Bath. The young kitchen lad had disappeared just as she knew he would, leaving her alone here save for the older cook who stayed in the kitchen and seldom ventured up to the second floor. It suited her, this state of things, because she had no one to answer to, no one to have to worry about. Such freedom was a rare prize and she still had days left before anyone returned. She could barely believe the luxury of it and on Monday she would go to the ball.

Leaving her bed, she began to pace around her room for the rhythm of walking always helped her, making her connection to the world stronger, the numbness less threatening. She felt her arms swing, not too far but far enough, matching her legs, bringing her body into the moment.

Normal people did not have such rituals, she knew that of course, but for her they brought her back from the abyss, made her calmer and allowed her to cope.

These were all the oddities Mr Rushworth had no notion of and never would. She liked that he found her interesting and different in a manner that was acceptable and there was no way in the world she wanted him to find out the true depths of her aberrations.

She would never fit in as he imagined—with him or with society. She rubbed at her sore leg and kept walking.

* * *

Bram Baker-Hill, Tobias Balcombe and Rupert Forsythe all turned up that evening, bringing with them copious bottles of brandy and a pile of meat pies procured from a street seller in Covent Garden.

'You've been difficult to get hold of, August, so we've come to find you. It seems we have years of news to catch up on and brandy should help with the talking.'

Tobias Balcombe uncorked the first bottle and crossed over to the small armoire in one corner of the library.

'I presume this is the drinks cabinet. I can't remember us ever coming here when we were young.'

'That's because we didn't.'

'Well, your brother was a bastard and your father wasn't much better, so if they were here then it's no wonder we were elsewhere.'

Bramwell had drawn seats from all the corners of the room and with the smell of the food and the laughter of his companions August felt transported back to the old school days, a group of friends at his side and everything right with the world.

'Tobias says you're looking for a place to settle?'

Rupert asked this as the others nodded. So they were not beating around the bush.

'I am.' He took a large sip of the excellent brandy before going on. 'I was thinking of somewhere to the north of London in the country.'

'Don't you already have land in that direction, August? Your grandmother left you her estate, didn't she?'

'She did, but I've come home from India to start a new life away from any reminder of family.'

'I thought your years out east were happy ones, August?' Everyone looked interested in hearing an answer to Rupert's query.

'Some were.'

When the truth of this settled Bram stood and raised his glass.

'Then it's damn good you are home again and we have all missed you being here. The Langham girl seemed mightily captivated by you at the Allans' ball the other night, as were a whole assortment of other young hopefuls. There is talk of the Bambury daughter, too. I remember your family hoped you might form a union with hers. Something about the lands that could be united, if I recall it rightly, and she is still unmarried?'

'I'm not here for marriage, Bram. Once was enough.'

'I would imagine, however, that as you are the new heir to the title your grandfather will have an opinion on such a stance.' Tobias's voice was as soft as it always had been.

'You are right, he does, but I do not want to be beholden to him.'

'Your family was always a difficult one, August, which is why boarding school saved you to some extent. It's also why it was a hell of a shock for us to find you had just disappeared. Here one day and gone the next.'

'I wrote a few letters...'

'With nothing in them. No explanation. There you

were in the East India Company in foreign parts and without a reasonable explanation and rumours abounding that you boarded the ship taking you there in an unfit state and without free will?'

'That's true. My grandfather found me passage and bundled me off.'

Those words settled into silence and he could tell that each of his friends had their suppositions about what had happened, but he was not ready to relate the events leading up to his departure just yet. He wanted peace and he wanted easiness. Besides, there was only so much malevolence one could joke about, he supposed, and his friends had probably reached their limit.

Bram opened the next bottle of brandy and dished out the rest of the meat pies. 'Eat them while they're hot, for I swear to you it's better fare than any kitchen in the land might deliver.'

And he was right, for the brandy and the spiced beef had some sort of taste that went together better than anything. The world began to look more whole to August, the company of good friends encouraging an honesty that he had not felt in years, except for just recently with Miss Euphemia Denniston.

Mia. She would like these people and she would fit in here with her own brand of truthful directness. Her bravery was a part of it, too. She did not allow others to define her because she genuinely did not care if they liked her or not. He wondered what she had thought of the golden dress adorned in pearls. Had she tried it on? Her short note had proffered polite thanks and that was about it.

When he had read it on the return of his servants he'd wondered if she would even honour her promise.

'There is another reason we are here today, August. Rupert thought his sister might appreciate you as an escort for the Barretts' ball. You remember her? An even-tempered girl and one who would not expect too much from you. Such an arrangement might allow you more liberty to look around and choose for yourself.'

'Thank you for the thought, but I have promised to escort somebody already.'

Shock kept the room quiet.

'Miss Euphemia Denniston.'

'The girl you carried into the side chamber at the Allans' ball the other night? The one in the old blue dress? The one you asked us about when you arrived?' Tobias's voice was alight with interest.

'The same one. She is the stepdaughter of Mrs Lucille Denniston.'

The name did not register on any of his friends' faces.

'I met Miss Denniston the day I docked in London when the Frost Fair was in full swing. Her stepmother was unwell so I offered her my carriage and when I saw her again at the Allans' ball we struck up a friendship.'

'She looked rather…sad.' Rupert's words were spoken in a hesitant way.

'That was because she'd come as a chaperon for her

stepsister and was wearing a gown that was well past its best. Tomorrow she will be there in her own right.'

'You think a woman like that will ward off the swathe of young girls who have taken such an interest in you?'

'I hope so.'

'As a sentinel or a guard? Does she know this is what you require of her?'

Before Augustus could find an appropriate answer, Tobias began to speak. 'She sounds unusual, which is a good thing, but the trick will be to hope she is not wanting more from you.'

'She has told me that she is as little interested in marriage as I am.'

'My wife is bound to like her, then.'

This time they all laughed.

'Good. But may I ask yet another favour of you all? Would you introduce her to your wives, for I doubt Euphemia knows many people at all in society?'

'She is important to you?'

'She is. If I can get through the next six weeks unscathed and unattached, I should be able to do just as I want.'

'And your grandfather would be put in his place?'

'The lure of Amerleigh House is strongest when the gambler has nothing left to bet with. But I hold a full hand. The title will be mine by law and the estate along with it, but my grandfather's personal fortune is something of which I have no need. I think he may have realised this fact the other day when he came down to London to visit.'

'So he can no longer hold the sword of Damocles above your head?'

Bram's question made him laugh.

'He can't.'

'You know he will require at least an heir from you, though?'

'A duty which I will honour in a few years' time when I am ready.'

'Hence the custodianship of Miss Euphemia Denniston? Well, here's to her then, your mysterious temporary watchwoman on sentry duty.'

The talk turned to the ten years lost between them and of the larger scandals that had rocked society since he'd last been among them. It was good to be in their company again, for they had been through much as boys and, even when separated by an ocean, had remained intricately bound together. He wished Tony Ferris could have been here, too, though he imagined he would see him as soon as he returned to London.

In India he had had friends, but none like these four. Bombay had demanded he be a different man, the constant risks there seldom allowing for any ease of tension. Jane had added to that, but Alice had sweetened the difficulties.

Alice again. She came to him at many odd moments almost every day, a quiet presence coated in a sadness that was all encompassing. A lost child in a dangerous continent at the end of an era. A family destroyed first by betrayal, the second in sickness.

Augustus no longer trusted in permanence, so the company of his friends was joyful and heartfelt.

Lord Rupert Forsythe entered his wife's dressing room just as she was dabbing on a few drops of her particular scent from a bottle on the table before retiring to bed.

Josephine turned on her stool and reached up to place her hands about his neck as he leaned down.

'You smell like brandy,' she teased and waited as he kissed her full on the lips. 'And you taste like it, too.'

'I've been at August Rushworth's house with Bram and Tobias and he implied he was escorting a lady to the Barretts' ball who has agreed to be his bodyguard.'

His wife frowned. 'In what way?'

'In the way of protecting him from all the unmarried girls who rushed him at the Allans' the other night.'

'Yes, that was rather noticeable, but then he is undeniably handsome.'

He kissed her again.

'Not as handsome as you are, my love, but close. I hope this woman knows what she might be in for. Is she large?'

'No. She is small, pale and rather frightened-looking from memory.'

'Intriguing?'

'Her gown appeared as if it was many sizes too large on her.'

'The mystery deepens.'

'The thing is that August asked if I would introduce you to her and I am certain he is wanting you to be kind.'

'When am I not, my love?'

'In bed sometimes…'

She laughed and stood. 'What is the girl's name?'

'Miss Euphemia Denniston. And she is not a girl. I doubt you would remember her.'

'But you do?'

'When she first came out she created a turmoil because she was both beautiful and sensible, though she was a year or so older than us, so this comes to me via my brother's tales. It is said she had many suitors.'

'I am beginning to like her more.'

'She disappeared from society after only a couple of weeks and didn't return until a few years ago, and as a very sorry version of the former siren.'

'The small, pale, old and frightened version?'

'I cannot understand what August would see in her to entrust such a position to.'

'Remember when you first saw me, Rupert? Remember that very first time?'

'When you were crying in the street after falling from the carriage?'

'With mud all over my face and a scratch down the side of my cheek?'

'I thought you were beautiful.'

'Exactly.'

He held her close for a moment and wondered just how he had been so lucky to find her.

'So you will seek her out and make her feel welcome?'

'Just you try to stop me.'

This time when she kissed him the feel of her body pressed against his own made him draw in a quick breath. She could arouse him so easily.

'I have been waiting for you, Rupert.'

Standing, she removed the dressing gown she was wearing and unpinned her hair. It fell in a silken blonde wave all the way down her naked back.

With ease he lifted her up and strode towards the bed, glad to see the covers had been turned and a candle had been lit.

Her smile told him she knew exactly what he wanted and he thanked God again for her presence in his life.

'August needs a wife as beautiful and as generous as you are, Josephine.'

'And perhaps, Rupert, he has found one?'

Then there was no more talking at all.

Chapter Five

Everything was done and she was ready, although the woman reflected in the mirror before her was a stranger. By a trick of magic, the lady's maid sent by Augustus Rushworth had conjured up this changeling, this woman glowing in gold and smiling as though she meant it.

Her hair was fashioned *à la Grecque* to the left side of her head and fastened in a full knot. A small lace cap sat above it decorated in tiny pearls.

Mia had had no idea of what was required to appropriately style all her finery before this afternoon, but Tilly, the maid, was talkative and knowledgeable, and more than willing to impart every small thing she knew about the proper dressing of a lady.

'You are beautiful, Miss Denniston. You are the most beautiful lady I have ever had the pleasure of dressing and that's saying something for in my time I've worked for many a fine family.'

'But you're now working for Mr Rushworth?' Mia

could not understand the connection, given Augustus Rushworth's recent arrival here in London and his lack of a wife.

'Oh, no, miss. I work for Lady Balcombe, who is the wife of one of his very close friends. Lady Balcombe sent me here today and instructed me to do my very best.'

'Well, I am most grateful for all your time, attention and knowledge, Tilly.'

The woman was tidying up her things now and re-packing combs and creams and powders. The rouge she had applied to Mia's lips made her mouth look wanton, but she did not dare to rub it off in front of her after such effort.

She heard the clock strike nine in the hallway and then there was a knock at the door. Fortunately, Bobby, the kitchen lad, had returned and she waited while he answered it and then came up to announce the arrival of Mr Rushworth.

Tilly stood back waiting and, with nothing else to put off the moment, Euphemia started down the staircase, making certain to hold on tightly to the banister, the golden gown swishing around her legs.

Augustus Rushworth stood very still as she came towards him, so still that Mia thought for a moment he was displeased. His eyes clamped on her, the darkness of his hair unbroken even under the light.

He was all in black tonight save for the white cravat at his neck, a colour that made him look dark and more distant.

Reaching him finally, she stood on the stair above so that their eyes met on a level.

'You are beautiful.'

She savoured the words, each one warming her, for the truth was there on his face. He looked like a man who did not lie.

'Thank you, sir, for everything.' Her hands gestured to the dress. 'I shall be very careful not to mark the satin.'

'The gown is yours to keep, Miss Denniston. I do not require its return.'

'I have never owned anything so expensive.'

'Well, you should have,' was all he said, the anger in his eyes visible now. It turned the caramel flecks to a darker brown and the feeling of protection there was so unfamiliar that it warmed her.

The lady's maid the Balcombes had sent hurried past, leaving them alone, and Mia felt as though they were strangers dressed in their finery, different people, and ones she hardly recognised.

'The maid you sent was astonishingly good at what she does. I barely recognise myself.'

'Anna Balcombe lent her to me for the day. Her husband, Tobias, is a good friend of mine. You will meet them tonight.'

August could not believe the transformation that a bit of gold material and a different hairstyle had wrought upon Miss Euphemia Denniston. Now it was going to be

even harder to impress on others that she was a friend
and that he was not on the marriage market.

Euphemia looked unbelievable, her hair containing
all the tints of blonde pulled up in a complicated knot
to one side, her neck a thin, pale column above a bodice that he found he wanted to hitch up to cover more
of the swell of her breasts. She was elegant and fragile,
the golden sheath that encased her body showing off
both her figure and her colouring.

His next thought was that he should have insisted
Anna choose a gown that was less revealing, something
that covered her more. At least her mother's pearls at
her neck did a little of that job, but the unmarked white
surface of her skin was tantalising because where it
fell down into the swell of her breast he could see how
well-endowed she was, ripe curves catching both his
attention and his ire.

He saw then that she watched him, her long lashes
darker and her lips redder than he remembered.

She was like a butterfly emerging from a chrysalis,
changed and bold, and knowing how well she looked.
There was something sensual in the conversion, something dark and strong.

God, what was he thinking? He swallowed and felt
for the box in his jacket pocket, bringing it out and
handing it to her.

'I thought they might match.' They were not the
words he had meant to give her at all; they were flip-
pant and defensive and held no mention of anything
more than expediency.

She took the package and opened it, her mouth forming a response.

'I could not accept these, Mr Rushworth. Not from you.'

The pearl earrings that were nestled in their green baize bed caught the light, the ancient treasures of the Amerleigh estate looking every bit as substantial as their worth. His mother had owned them once and they had come to him now, along with a drawer full of other priceless trinkets locked in the safe at the town house, just waiting for someone to wear them.

'Think of them as a loan, then.' He could not for the life of him insist otherwise because her appearance had thrown him so far off kilter that everything he uttered he now questioned.

Relief flooded her blue eyes, which were the colour of cornflowers in the summer, a hint of purple at their edges. Every tiny piece of her was magnified tonight and made brighter.

'Did these come from Lady Balcombe, too?'

'No.'

He found he couldn't explain further and he suddenly needed a drink, badly.

'I will be most careful with them, Mr Rushworth, for they look truly magnificent.'

She put on the gold-and-pearl earrings, but she did not cross to the mirror to look at herself as any other woman would undoubtedly have done. She simply stood there, her arms at her sides, her décolletage prettily flushed. He wished they were not going to a crowded ball. He wished he could take her back to his house to dine and talk, to touch, perhaps, and feel the fullness of her curves. To take her to his bed and make love to her until the morning.

He gritted his teeth together.

Euphemia Denniston was attending the ball at his invitation and under the promise of being a buffer against all the young women who considered him worthy game on the matrimonial market. To turn the pledge into something else again would be unfair and unscrupulous.

He felt like a young lad again, confronted with the magnitude of her beauty, all at sea in a storm.

Regrouping, he took in a breath.

'Before we go there is something I need to tell you.'

Worry threaded across her face.

'When I left England ten years ago, I was essentially booted out by my family, but my father's death last year created a hole in the line of succession and so my grandfather called me home. We are not close and probably never will be, but I have a group of friends who were always like brothers to me and they will be with us tonight.'

'The Balcombes included?'

He nodded. 'They are good people.'

'Whom you trust?'

'I do.'

'Have you told them about our arrangement?'

'I told them a little, but not all.'

Her smile was tight. 'I hope they will like me.'

'Who would not, Euphemia?'

'Almost everyone I meet, nowadays. I think it is because of my station in life. People want to know someone much more interesting.'

'You sell yourself short with such doubt.'

But she was not finished. 'They want a person who is not afraid of life, a person who excites them.'

'Your honesty always astounds me.'

'But you are different, Mr Rushworth. You are so certain of everything that to have someone at your side who is sure of nothing will not be such a problem.'

This time he laughed out loud. 'Perception has its limitations, Euphemia.'

'Name one thing that worries you, then.'

He struggled to think of something off the top of his head.

'See, if you had asked *me* such a question I could recite all manner of things and in so great a list that you might wish you had never asked.'

'Do not think of them tonight. Just take a breath and smile and see where that gets you.'

'And you will stay by me.'

'Isn't that the plan?'

'Yes.'

'The earrings suit you.'

'Everything you have lent me is beautiful. You have excellent taste. My father, alas, had no taste at all, so our house is filled with things that have become uglier and uglier with the passing of time.' She looked around. 'Take that cabinet, for instance. Papa bought that from a man with a cart who was hawking things on the Whitechapel Road. The door has never worked and the carving upon it is so rough and ill-conceived that I doubt the craftsman spent much time on it at all.'

'I like the picture there.' His attention had been caught by a scene of a family sitting near a river with some animals before them drinking from the water.

'Oh, that is an old painting of my grandfather's. He was an Honourable something from somewhere up north.'

'You never met him?'

'My father cut ties with any family he had before I was born.'

'And regretted it?'

'I don't think so. It was my regret that was felt more sorely. I should have liked to know a cousin or an aunt or visit a house that had been part of the Denniston family for generations before.'

'You may not have missed as much as you imagine for family tradition can tie you down with its heavy needs. I want to find a property that is new and light and entirely my own.'

'To start your own traditions?'

He nodded. 'In India I lived in the middle of Bombay, a busy sea port in the Maharashtra Province, and I promised myself that if and when I returned to England my next home would be in an empty part of the countryside and far from any crowds.'

'And where is the estate of the Rushworth family?'

'Between Nantwich and Audley in Cheshire.'

'Which I am led to believe is also a lovely and empty part of the countryside and far from any crowds?'

He smiled at her repetition of his words. 'You haven't been there?'

'I've never been out of London, sir.'

August was astonished. She was the granddaughter of an Honourable and the daughter of a gentleman and yet she had never left the confines of the city? There were so many things about her that did not quite add up.

He wanted to step forward and take her in his arms. In truth, he wanted to turn her face up to his and kiss her, kiss the rouge from her lips until they were reddened from his own ministrations.

Hell. He could feel things inside himself that he had not felt for a long time, the quick rush of want and need, and it was worrying because there was fear stamped in her eyes.

Augustus Rushworth looked just like his brother had before he'd attacked her that night at the Dashwoods' ball, in the semi-dark, with the curtains to one side. The likeness was in his breathing and his stillness and in the intensity that magnified even as she watched him.

'I think we should go.' Her voice shook with alarm.

He frowned and stepped back. For the first time in his company, she thought he seemed uncertain.

'My carriage is waiting.'

He was silent as they left the house. He touched only her arm as he very lightly helped her in. Once there, he sat on the opposite seat from hers and looked out of the window.

Her thick navy cloak sealed her off from the world and she was glad of it. Something had changed between them and, where before there had been ease, now there was stiffness. She was just Miss Euphemia Denniston and he was next in line for a barony.

He'd wanted to kiss her. She had seen it in his face a moment ago, but not any more. She cursed herself for her stupidity in comparing him with his brother, though the fright of what might have happened was still with her. Lingering.

She needed to find her way through such dread because, if she didn't, she would always be this person: anxious and apprehensive and alarmed. And suddenly she didn't want to be that person any more. She had to trust him, had to have faith in his goodness, had to forge another connection that might break the terrible associations that bound her up into panic.

Breathing in, she let out the air slowly. Such ministrations helped her find a balance. She could not tell him of her past, but she could tell him of her hopes for the future.

'It has been a long while since I have been in the company of a man I liked.'

She watched him turn and look at her.

'You spoke to me of secrets once, Mr Rushworth, and of the fact that everyone hides something that they do not wish to dwell on, but you also asked me for honesty, so this is mine: every woman in the room tonight will wish that you might sweep them off their feet and kiss them. But I am not one of those women because… I am afraid of such a touch.'

'Afraid?'

She nodded and did not try to hide the depth of her feeling.

'If I asked why, Euphemia, I doubt you would tell me, but I will give you another promise. I would never hurt you, at least know that.'

'I do.'

The silence swelled in the darkness, a small warm space in a world of wind and rain, and she found her body relaxing because of it, because of him.

'I am grateful that you do not give up on me entirely and take me home.'

He smiled. 'Oh, you will find I am far more tenacious than that, Miss Denniston, and mystery has always fascinated me. Besides, to waste your beauty tonight on a secret from the past would be inexcusable and in that gown you deserve to be seen.'

Euphemia was never easy, he thought, even as she smiled back at him. There had never been one time since he had met her when he could have said, *Ah, now I know who she truly is.* No, she veered from talkative to silent and from straightforward to downright mysterious. Like the clothes she wore. At one time this and the next time that. From the drab, threadbare navy blue gown he had seen her in at the Allans' ball to the golden gown she now had on under a velvet cloak that had transformed her into a goddess.

It was part of her appeal, he thought next, because so far in his life the women he had been close to had always been simple to read. His wife, for example, had been either depressed or ecstatic and the few lovers he had taken after she had died had been at pains to say all the things they thought he might have wanted to hear.

Wealth helped smooth problems, he'd found, but Euphemia did not seem particularly swayed by such largesse, either. No, she'd taken the pearl earrings only as a loan and tried to give him back the dress.

He needed to earn her trust, needed to make her realise that perhaps she would like to be kissed. By him.

The thought had him sitting up straighter and he was relieved when he saw the lights from the Barretts' town house coming into view.

Chapter Six

If the Allans' ball had been a spectacle, then this one was twenty times more so, the decorations stellar, the rooms magnificent and the crowd of a size Mia could never in her life have imagined.

Everyone was here. And they all wanted to talk to the new heir of Rushworth, it seemed, the crowd around him bigger and bigger and the disgruntled faces of the beautiful younger women who were trying to distract him looking less and less sure as she remained by his side, her hand on his arm.

Just as she had promised. That was why she was here, after all.

But there were other things at play as well, because every time she looked up another man was trying to vie for her own attention, not one of the old, unhinged types that she sometimes swatted off at social occasions, but one of the younger variety, handsome men with ready compliments. It was surprising. It made her hand tighten on the sleeve of Augustus Rushworth's arm with an even greater purpose, for to be flung into the pool of men who might ask her to dance was a horror that did not bear thinking about.

And so they stood there, a bulwark against the push of hopefuls, smiling, talking, and all the time together.

'I cannot believe you have returned to us, Mr Rushworth, after all of these years.' A breathless debutante and her mother stood in front of them. 'Why, I was just talking with Mr Sedgwick and he was relaying a tale of seeing you out there in the wilds of India. Such a backward land by his accounts.'

'Well, everyone has their own opinion, Lady Baring. On my part I found it most enlightening.'

'Mr Sedgwick said you resided in one of the most beautiful parts of Bombay. He also said you were often away.'

'I was.'

Euphemia recognised a tone she had not heard before in his voice and his arm beneath her hand tensed. He did not like this Mr Sedgwick. She could feel that he did not.

'He also said your late wife was very beautiful?'

Mia stepped into the awkward silence with her own observation.

'Mr Rushworth, would you mind escorting me into the other salon? I have a friend waiting there.'

She smiled at the pair before her and was relieved when he moved away with her.

'I thought we had had enough of them,' she said as they went.

'It's all right, Euphemia. I can fight my own battles.'

They had stopped now and were looking at each other. She took in a breath as she answered.

'I know you can, but you should not always have to. You have helped me in a number of ways and it is only fair that I should help you in return.' Swallowing, she continued on. 'I have found through personal experience that the only approach to effectively deal with the barbs of gossip is to remove yourself from them.'

'A wise choice. I will endeavour to do the same.'

She could hear the humour in his voice and was glad of it. At least the anger was gone.

'I hope your friends are in the next salon.'

'Over there, near the third pillar.' He took her hand and led her towards them.

'August.' A tall man came forward first, a warm smile on his face. 'We thought you might be stuck in that melee for ever.' His eyes came across to her own in question.

'Miss Euphemia Denniston, meet Lord Balcombe. We were at school together and he is one of my oldest friends.'

'Pleased to meet you, Lord Balcombe, and I wish to thank your wife for her generosity in lending me her lady's maid for the afternoon.'

'A task that the maid was well up to, it seems. My wife, Anna, is just here.'

A tall, thin woman appeared behind him and she took Mia's hand in her own as her husband spoke to Augustus.

'You look wonderful, Miss Denniston. I knew you would suit this colour entirely after Rushworth described you.'

'You had something to do with the choosing of this dress?'

'Oh, of course, but it was a secret. You do not think August might have managed the task on his own, do you? No, he might be most competent in other things, but in the choosing of an evening dress...' She tailed off before beginning again. 'My husband and his friends are so thrilled to have him back because they have missed him and ten years is a long time to be gone. The very best thing about it all is that he seems happy, which, by all accounts, he was not when he left.'

They were interrupted then by the same man Euphemia had seen with Rushworth at the Allans' ball when she had fainted.

'It's good to see you looking so well, Miss Denniston. You have made quite the impression here tonight.'

'I had a lot of help.'

'Anna was telling us of her part in aiding August's scheme and her taste is as always impeccable. May I introduce my own wife to you?'

A very beautiful woman stepped up beside him and smiled. 'I am Christina Baker-Hill. My husband Bramwell told me about your misfortune the other night so I am very glad to see you recovered.'

Bramwell and Christina Baker-Hill. She had heard so much about this couple across the years, but never yet laid eyes on them in the flesh.

Augustus turned from his conversation with Lord Balcombe and moved in beside her, but among this company Mia was not sure if she should take his arm or not and so she didn't.

He solved the question entirely by finding her hand himself and repositioning it across his sleeve. She saw Bramwell Baker-Hill look over at his wife in surprise and her heartbeat quickened.

She did not wish to mislead these people, but if August needed her there...

August? She had not named him so familiarly before, even in her thoughts. A surge of warmth flooded in because tonight it had felt so natural to be in his company.

More usually, she was pushed aside or she was fleeing to somewhere private and watching the time for the first opportunity to leave. She could feel eyes upon her, but they did not worry her as they usually did. Tonight she was safe with him beside her and, if she had been thrown earlier when he had looked as if he had wanted to kiss her, now she was just thankful for his solidness beneath her fingers.

Rupert Forsythe and his wife were the final couple in this group and Mia warmed to Josephine Forsythe immediately; she looked a trifle flummoxed by all the people and slightly unsure of things. While her husband was tall and muscular, she was short and rounded, but when she spoke Euphemia easily understood her attraction.

'I have been wanting to meet with you, Miss Denniston. Anyone who puts a smile on the face of Rushworth is to be valued for it means he might stay put in England a while and I know my husband for one would very much like him to. Besides, Annabelle Langham and the other young, silly girls here have no place at all in his life with their constant chatter and mindless worries. It would simply not do to see him marry one of them. No, not at all.'

Her husband smiled as he heard her words. 'Josie has strong opinions, Miss Denniston, ones I hope shall not offend you.'

'Oh, quite the contrary, Mr Forsythe. Firm opinions always impress me because I would very much like to have them myself.'

'But you don't?' Josephine looked interested.

'She thinks she does not, but I have yet to discover this timid person Euphemia swears herself to be.'

Augustus had joined the conversation now and Mia was heartened by his words.

'Euphemia is a most unusual name.'

It was Anna Balcombe who noted this.

'I often use Mia instead, as it is easier. If you would prefer that one...'

Josephine Forsythe interrupted. 'Indeed not. *Euphemia and the Goth* is a text of Syriac literature that I read once in Greek and the miracle she encountered has always intrigued me.'

'Miracle?' Mia could not help but ask.

'The Divine Lord heard her prayer and transported her from inside her sealed tomb to safety. She made it home again to her loyal mother and lived happily ever after without the miserable husband who had imprisoned her there in the first place.'

'A tale of great fortune, then.' Augustus sounded as though he was amused.

'My wife rarely tells a story with an unhappy ending, August. You must at least remember that of her.' Rupert Forsythe looked as equally entertained.

'I do, Rupert, for when you were finding life difficult all those years ago you appreciated the fact that she could make you laugh.'

'A characteristic that is often undervalued, I might add.' Josephine was quick to join the conversation. 'Rupert and I will have been married for nine years next week and we have four children to show for it aged between one and seven. So he must enjoy my company as much as I enjoy his.'

Such conversation was easy, Mia thought. It seemed that any subject was appropriate for discussion and that opinions, divided or otherwise, were listened to.

She glanced at Augustus Rushworth and saw that he watched her, too, his eyes alight with humour.

'Would you dance with me, Euphemia?'

'I will.'

It was another waltz, she realised, though she had not heard the tune until she was closer to the dance floor. When he took her in his arms she found herself leaning in, pleased for his warmth and his size. He was a sanctuary among the masses and a place to feel whole.

'I like your friends,' she said as they moved into the steps. 'It must be wonderful to have people in your life who are always just there, people who you can pick up again without difficulty after so long.'

'You haven't any like that?'

'No.' She said it with a conviction that was startling.

'Josephine came from a family of wandering minstrels. Rupert met her when she was injured on the streets after falling from a carriage one cold winter morning and he offered her help.'

'So she is not…from society?'

'God, no. Neither is Anna Balcombe. She was a country girl when Tobias met her on a trip up to the Balcombe estates and her mother was a seamstress in a small rural town.'

'And Christina Baker-Hill?'

'Well, she is the daughter of a duke.'

'A disparate lot, then.' She laughed. 'Which school did you all attend?'

'Eton.'

That knocked her back a little because everyone knew of the cost of an education like that.

'Hardly penniless, then.'

'Looks can be deceiving. Most of our fathers were hanging on to family estates by their fingernails because none had the sense to invest in the burgeoning industrial age. They thought it beneath them.'

'A penchant you seem to have remedied by acquiring a fortune?'

'Well, I stuck to trade, which was even more distasteful in the eyes of many.'

'I like that you did. You smelt lovely that first day I met you. Like buns at Christmas.'

He laughed loudly and lost his step, and as she was pulled towards him a sharp ache ran down her thigh.

'Does your leg pain you, Miss Denniston? I have noticed you favouring it.'

That took her back and all ease faded.

Another misstep, he thought.

He felt her there beside him, pale and thin and injured in some way, but striving to be braver.

Euphemia Denniston had made sure she was next to him for the entire night, her hand on his sleeve and a barrier against everyone else. The quiet reminder of her care warmed him and he hoped he was doing the same for her.

She looked to be enjoying the evening, laughing with his friends and moving closer to him in the dance. He'd felt the slight movement of her breath against his face when he'd dipped down to listen to what she said. It was not often that he'd felt so content. In fact, he could not remember when he last had been this happy and that was despite her telling him that she did not wish to be kissed.

A puzzle of so many pieces.

He took smaller steps until they danced on the spot, on the edge of the space by the floor-to-ceiling windows, snow flurries against the glass.

But he didn't feel cold.

'You are by far the most interesting woman in this room, Miss Euphemia Denniston.'

She glanced up and he saw a smile flutter around her mouth.

'If I could have one wish, I would like it to be that.'

'And the most beautiful.'

'That is not quite so believable, Mr Rushworth, and besides it is a dangerous thing.'

'How so?'

'Beauty can only disappoint you when it fades.'

His hand tightened across hers and he was pleased when she did not pull away. It was a small caress hidden from the eyes of strangers and only between them, the music of Mozart lilting and poignant. He was suddenly struck with the rightness of it all, of her in his arms, of his laughter and his comfort, of their small bubble away from others, sealed in a satisfaction that was astonishing.

He had never felt like this before. Breathing in slowly, he tried to balance himself and when she looked up the blue in her eyes was so clear and true that he was lost in it.

'Come with me for a drive tomorrow. I will take you outside of London and show you the countryside.'

'And the snow?'

'It makes it even better and we will stop somewhere for lunch.'

A whole day in her company. He'd not made plans with any woman for so long and was again amazed that he had offered such a suggestion.

'It would be just us?'

'It will be, but wear warm clothes because it's sure to be cold.'

The last flourish of the music was upon them and then the dance was finished, the small orchestra stopping for a break as supper was called.

As Rupert and Bram walked towards them with all the others behind, Augustus knew the time of just himself and Euphemia was over. He tucked her hand into the crook of his arm as they went to meet them.

Supper was sumptuous and set out over myriad tables in a large room off the front salons, each one laden with food. Augustus Rushworth brought her over to the place where they were to sit and pulled out her chair.

'The Barretts always excel at the seating plan for a supper,' Rupert Forsythe said as he and his wife took their seats opposite. 'They don't place disparate people together in an attempt at fostering conviviality, but stick to the recipe of tried and true friendship instead, which is a relief.'

Mia had never been to such an affair and the few balls she had attended had not had a seated meal as part of the programme.

'Did you know Augustus before he went to India, Miss Denniston?'

Anna Balcombe, beside her, asked this question.

'Oh, please do call me Mia and, no, I did not. I was only out in society briefly, you see.'

'You did not stay a whole Season?'

'No. Just a few weeks. It was enough.'

The same feelings of panic that she felt whenever she thought about that time resurfaced and she forced herself to smile. She could tell that Augustus was listening in to this conversation, too, which made things worse again.

But Rupert Forsythe was speaking now, as he recited a story about the boys at school all those years before which caught the attention of everyone.

'We'd gone up to my father's house for the holidays, the summer one it must have been because I remember it was hot. Tony Ferris was with us, too, and you will no doubt meet him in the next week or so, Miss Denniston. Anyway, Bram insisted we all build a raft and cross the river at the bottom of the property, and quite a wide river it was, too. August asked us if we could swim and we told him we could for we knew he was a strong swimmer. But the truth was we were all hopeless, so when the raft began to sink mid-river it was up to him to jump in and tow us across to safety, which would have been fine had a large timber pole not come undone and fallen on top of him, clouting him on the head.'

'And the blood, Rupert.' Tobias interjected. 'Remember that. He bled so much the water around us was red and by the time he got us back to the bank he was freezing.'

'My father was furious when we got home and we were all sent to our rooms without supper, save for August, who was given twenty stitches by the local doctor.'

Laughter ensued.

'But we all survived and after that you lot learnt to swim so it was a happy ending.' Mia could hear the humour in Augustus's voice.

'Have you still got the scar, August?' Bramwell Baker-Hill asked this of him.

'Probably.' His hand went to the back of his head and he felt around for it. 'It was the haircut the doctor gave me that I hated the most because they called me Blackbeard the pirate for months afterwards until it grew back.' He addressed this to her, a rueful tone in his voice.

'The rules for boys seem different than they were back then. Nowadays no one does anything even slightly dangerous.' Tobias Balcombe raised his drink. 'Here's to your return, August. We have missed you.'

Sitting watching them, Euphemia had the impression that Augustus must have been quite the leader of the pack, just as he was now, quieter than the others, but strong somehow. She liked that about him, this calm competence, a man who might deal with anything thrown his way.

She felt him next to her, his leg only a few inches to one side of hers. If she moved slightly, she might touch him…

Taking a sip of her orange drink, she stayed still. What was she thinking? The boundaries of her friendship with Mr Rushworth had been well and truly set and for all the years of her life and especially since the dreadful incident at the Dashwoods' ball she had been most cautious of any man. If this one was different, then she needed to be more careful again, because he had wanted her help for a month, nothing more.

She was glad when the food was served and she could concentrate on that rather than on the unsettling presence of Augustus Rushworth.

'Are you enjoying yourself, Euphemia?'

His smile was wide as he asked this, their small pocket of privacy welcome as they began to eat.

'Very much so.'

The words between them were banal, but as his eyes locked in to her own she blushed. Every woman in the room was watching him and she was aware of the constant scrutiny for a very public outing countenanced no mistakes.

She could not drop her guard and allow an error to catch them out, for it was he she was protecting, too. The mouse and the lion. That thought made her smile.

'Do you believe in karma, Euphemia?'

'You mean good luck and bad luck?'

'Well, in Hinduism karma is the belief that the sum of a person's actions in this life determines their fate in any future existences.'

'Like an enticement?'

'Or a disincentive. My ancestors would have done well to take notice of such a premise.'

'They didn't?'

He laughed. 'How did we get on to such a maudlin topic in the middle of a ball?'

'Karma,' she answered and something leapt between

them. Like fire, she was to think later, glittering as diamonds and winding heat into every corner of her body.

'Damn,' he swore and dragged his eyes from her own, his hand shaking as he lifted his fork, but at that moment Rupert Forsythe turned towards Augustus and began to speak, leaving her to sit in shock. Listening to the words without gathering meaning, she smiled at Anna Balcombe on the other side of the table, trying to find some normality in the sheer oddity of what had just happened.

The risk of it all made her feel fluid, a vessel of a thousand feelings and an impossible choice. Her reactions to her imagined dream lover were only a poor and pale rendition of what she felt now, Augustus Rushworth alive and large sitting next to her, his skin under the lights sun-touched and his hair the darkest of blacks. Without his gloves on, she could see the web of light scars across his fingers reaching up on to the wrist of his right hand. He wore such jeopardy like a banner, a man to be careful of, an unknown man, a man who would not be moulded into any shape or form apart from the one he wanted to take.

It was so far from her own life and experience.

She could barely swallow any food, her mouth dry with the breathless deceit she was immured in and the certain knowledge of her own failings. She felt like an ash tree balanced in the wind, tossed this way and that by all the currents of air, no control in any of it.

He moved and his leg came against hers, the warmth of it felt through the thin fabric of her golden gown.

Nothing else existed around her save for that touch, unintentional probably on his part, but startling on hers.

This night wasn't as she had expected it to be, the formality of a very large ball transformed into small miniatures of delight and feeling.

They danced again after supper and it was another waltz.

She had done her best to shelter him from the worst of the young women and their pushy mothers, but even then a few of the more adamant ones had slipped through to confront him. Mia had admired his composure and his patience and smiled as he had manoeuvred them away when he had had enough, for the victory of her protection was a heady elixir.

Even now as the crowd had thinned, she saw how people watched him and how he confounded them with his careful veils of ambiguity. No one here really knew him—she did not either—and even his friends who harked back to old adventures must have wondered about who he had become after ten years away in an exotic and unknown place.

The silver bracelet with the strange markings caught her eye where it had slipped from its tether beneath his cuff. It symbolised him, she thought, the shrouds of history in the hot lands of the Far East, the colour and the danger, the easy and the hard.

She wanted to ask him about the bracelet, but something stopped her, a reticence that was born from his own distance. She could dance with him and talk with him, and he could want to kiss her or not, but there was always something held back. Something important and elemental, something that she had seen even as he laughed with his old friends.

This world was his, but he had not wanted it, just as he had not wanted to stay in India. Where was his place? she wondered, she who had never had a true home anywhere. It was astonishing that he had thrown it all away so nonchalantly.

'You look deep in thought.'

'You manage your world easily, sir. Far more easily than I have ever managed mine. I should have liked to be able to look back and have seen things in the last ten years that were…magnificent.'

'You think that of me?'

'When you spoke with your friends about the places you have seen in India, I thought of how different we are. I find books that might tell of such foreign shores, but you actually go there and know it.'

'The grass is always greener where one has not been…'

'You are saying it is not as others think?'

'I am saying that dancing with you here with your dimples on show is exactly where I want to be, right now.'

'Always the diplomat, Mr Rushworth.'

'Or a man who speaks the truth, Euphemia? You decide.'

She liked it when he used her name like this, rolling it off his tongue like music. She liked the way he smiled at her, too.

'When I am old I will remember this moment as something wonderful,' she said.

'So far away? Why not live for now, for this minute?'

'Is that what you do?'

'I try.'

But she had seen the darkness in him before he could hide it, a sadness without limit, a rip that exposed all the things he did not say.

'Stay with me tonight. Come home with me.'

She could not believe he would ask this of her in a crowded ballroom, whispered a foot away from others.

'I can't.'

He only nodded and pulled her closer, their bodies sharing strength and their hands held tight. A magic that was indescribable and sad.

He smelt of musk and a good quality soap, the spices on him at the dock gone now to be replaced by the scents of an aristocratic English lord. She breathed him in, to remember.

He thought her brave, but she wasn't.

He thought her whole, but she was broken.

And there was no way in the world that she could tell him how to fix her because she did not know how to do that herself.

As they left the dance floor, a man stood in their way, a tall man whom others would probably describe as handsome, but whom Euphemia could only describe as arrogant.

'I need to explain things, Rushworth, and you have not returned any of my letters the past few days.'

'And did you wonder why not, Sedgwick?'

Now Augustus was not even trying to be polite.

'Jane was lonely. She said you were never there and that her life was one of emptiness. She needed someone to be there for her.'

'I don't want to hear this, especially not here. Get out of my way.'

But the man only stepped forward, his voice lowering as he saw the interest their meeting was garnering. 'When she died, a part of me died, too.'

'Damn you,' Augustus Rushworth said and then added something in another language and Mia thought perhaps this Sedgwick understood it for he paled and turned away.

Then he was gone and they were past him, a smile pasted across Augustus's face as he acknowledged those around him.

The carriage ride home was awkward. Augustus sat on one side and she sat on the other, the heavy blanket of wool tucked in across her lap.

They had not danced again after the meeting with Sedgwick and Augustus had withdrawn, leaving her with his friends as he spoke with others at a distance, the young women surrounding him not such a nuisance now, his laughter easily heard as they flirted with him for all that they were worth.

When he had returned to her side after an hour, it

was to ask whether she wanted to leave and, sensing his desire to be gone, she had acquiesced.

The magic had dissipated and worry now sat in her stomach like a congealed fear, one which all the grandeur of the garments he had found for her still failed to change.

She lacked bravery and determination. She allowed others to define her and she acquiesced at the first sign of trouble. It was the only way she had managed to survive and she couldn't alter it, couldn't become the siren he may have liked, the woman who would have agreed to going home with him and spending the night. The small thought that she might have said yes if he had asked her at the table with his leg against her own made her ashamed, for lust had been her undoing years ago and she had vowed never to repeat such stupidity.

When he saw her to the door she did not ask him in.

'Thank you, Mr Rushworth.'

Bobby was there then, beside her, the young kitchen lad surprisingly well turned out.

'I shall see you inside, Miss Denniston.'

When she nodded, Augustus left, walking across the wet ground with the wind in his hair.

He did not look back.

He should have hit Sedgwick, right then and there, in the ballroom under the lights with a hundred people next to him. He should have pummelled his gloating face into the ground and knocked his damn teeth out, but instead...instead he had let the bastard get to him with his empty innuendoes and his shallow betrayals. And all that resentment had led to where he was now, in his carriage going home without seeing Euphemia inside or saying goodnight properly.

Probably with her intellect she had deduced that he had been a neglectful and an inattentive husband. His wife had been unfaithful nearly all the years of their marriage, sleeping with this person and flirting with that one. Lance Sedgwick, with his flowery compliments and his English sense of honour, just had not seen it coming.

Jane had died before the man had known who she really was, died after a pointless affair with a businessman acquaintance from the eastern coast who had come to her bed carrying the cholera and infected all the rest of her family. Their family.

He balled his fist and slammed it down on his knee, refusing just at this moment to even think about Alice.

The whole second half of the night had been a disaster. Why the hell had he asked Euphemia to come home with him and stay the night? What on earth had made him blurt out such an invitation in the middle of a dance floor and to a woman who was only just beginning to know him? He had never been so socially hopeless before, so desperate he'd hardly thought about the possibility of her saying no.

But no she had said and now he was left trying to pick up the pieces and bind them into some sort of satisfactory whole. He had wanted her so much to say yes and therein lay the trouble.

Running his fingers through his hair, he breathed out hard, because he wondered if she would even want to see him again.

Euphemia stood inside the door, her back against the wood as she listened to his carriage leave.

He was angry. Angry at her and at Mr Sedgwick and at his dead wife as well, she thought, the one who was lonely and left at home while all the duties of his job with the East India Company pulled him away.

Sedgwick had loved her, that much was obvious, but she knew that there were always two sides to any story. His lost wife must have made a mistake and been unfaithful just as she herself had made mistakes all those years ago at the Dashwoods' ball.

Disaster was never a simple recipe of honour and blame. It incorporated deceit and luck, both good and bad, and if fate sometimes brought fortune it could also just as easily bring ruin.

It was why she never took an alcoholic drink under any circumstance and why she stayed in full view of the crowd at every social occasion. It was why she feared touch and expected treachery even when she herself stuck to the path of honesty with such a steadfast purpose.

It was all the small bits of her glued together after her ruin, desperately trying to find the whole she had once been before…

Shaking her head, she stepped away from the door,

watching as Bobby came back from wherever he had been and turned the lock on it.

'Goodnight, miss,' he said with a smile. 'I will see to the lights.'

'Thank you.'

She was home and safe, all the highs and lows of the night setting her on edge and making her feel slightly sick. She remembered this feeling and breathed hard, counting, in, hold, out. Again and again she repeated it until the panic seemed lessened and she could walk up the stairs to her room, swinging her arms, this way and that, her legs matching the movement.

Once there she looked at herself in the mirror, surprised to see composure and poise reflected back, a woman on the outside who did not reflect all the anxious churnings on the inside.

A secret person who hid the veils of her past, the shame obscured and the fury suppressed.

The gold dress glowed in the light as she removed the wool cloak to leave the white fullness of the curves of her breasts ample and noticeable.

He had said that to her then, all those years ago, that she was made for sex and that pain should be mingled with pleasure, his hands reaching for and unleashing her flesh from the fabric of her green silk gown.

Swallowing, she looked away and took up a nightdress of thick wool that she could button tightly right up to her neck.

Chapter Seven

She dreamed that night of all that had been, a startling wholly formed memory that pounced upon her as soon as she fell asleep.

'Are you certain this looks well on me?' she had asked of Lucille as she'd peered into the mirror at the dress her father had purchased a week or two before. 'It seems too...bare, somehow?'

Lucille shook her head. 'Your father would be most put out should you make a fuss about the clothes. It is a big expenditure, after all, and he was most pleased to find these when he did.'

Euphemia glanced over at the two other gowns lying on her bed, both with necklines slightly higher than this one.

'Whitechapel seems a strange place to have found them,' she said quietly, but Lucille would have none of it.

'The vendor was a gentleman who was down on his luck, your father said, a man who needed ready cash and was prepared to sell them at a good price. This is your chance to shine, Euphemia, to find a husband of wealth and live a life that is comfortable. Lionel is getting older, after all, and does not need the worry of a dependent daughter upon his shoulders and you are seventeen, which is well past time for you to find a good life of your own.'

Duty. It crouched beside her like a big black obligation and Mia wished she could simply disappear into the country somewhere and live a life that was her own entirely. The two balls she had already attended had been stuffy, interminable affairs where the men had talked constantly and expected very little in the way of conversation back from her.

She looked at herself in the mirror again.

The green of the gown was bolder than the colour of the other two gowns she had already worn, a colour that did not quite suit her, she thought, the yellowish undertone of it clashing with the gold in her hair. She tried to pull up the fabric at the neckline over the plumpness of her breasts. This dress was far tighter than the other ones, but there was little she could do about it now.

'Use the assets you have to snare a husband, Euphemia. That would be my advice to you, for beauty soon fades and then there is nothing of it left and you will be on the shelf for ever.' Lucille's voice was harsh and, taking a deep breath, Mia picked up her reticule and followed her stepmother out of the room.

Mr Jeremy Rushworth asked her to dance almost as soon as she arrived. She had met him the previous week at the first ball she had attended, though only very briefly.

'It is good to see you again, Miss Denniston. I'd hoped you would be here tonight.'

She felt his hand tighten on her own and blushed.

'The gown you wear is very flattering,' he went on and his eyes fell to the neckline with a sort of fervency. 'Of all the girls here, you are the most mysterious for no one knows exactly who you are.'

'There is no secret, Mr Rushworth. I have lived in London all my life with my father. I think people like to confuse anonymity with the clandestine, the suitable thrill of chance, if you like, which makes no sense at all.'

'A bluestocking, too? I enjoy a woman with a sharp mind.'

'Do you?'

'Indeed. The boredom of life is most prevalent in places such as this and to find someone with whom you can have a real conversation is…well, it is unusual. At Amerleigh House, my extensive family estate in Cheshire, we have a well-stocked library.'

The evening was shaping up, Euphemia thought, a partner who liked books and one who allowed a woman to have opinions.

'My grandfather, Baron Rushworth of Amerleigh, feels literature to be important and this is something he has instilled in the family—the love of a story and the world that it brings to one. I pity people who do not read for they have lost the chance of wonder.'

'What do you like to read, sir?'

'Everything. I could not pick one tome that I like above the others. That would be like having to choose a favoured child and I most certainly could not do that.'

He was laughing now and with the lights above and the music around them, Euphemia felt a shift in her perceptions of these affairs. With the right partner, perhaps these balls could be marvellous things, full of energy and discovery and excitement.

'I love the theatre, too. Do you attend it much, Miss Denniston?'

When she shook her head he carried on. 'Then I shall take you to the Lyceum in Wellington Street and we will see all the great plays of the day and afterwards we shall eat by candlelight and discuss our thoughts till the small hours of the morning. Would you like to do that?'

'I am not sure,' she said as the music wound down to the end of the dance, for it all sounded rather wanton and loose. When a waiter with a silver tray full of elegant thin-stemmed glasses appeared, her partner took two and handed her one, quickly finishing his own and waiting for her to do the same before finding two more in quick succession.

'Come, we will stand over there by the long windows and look out into the night, for it has just started to snow and it is a magical sight.'

Threading through the throng, they arrived in a place of quietness, a small alcove allowing them some privacy.

'To you, Miss Denniston, and to beauty.' He finished

his wine and glanced pointedly at her own. 'Drink up, my love, for there are plenty more where these came from.'

His endearment was odd, but the wine had made her less worried somehow, so she did as he asked. When he excused himself for a moment he returned to her with a third offering.

'Three is a lucky number,' he said.

Euphemia felt a little disorientated and she could feel the front of her dress dipping even lower. She saw his eyes on her breasts again, a new interest there which was sharpened by strong libation. She could feel the warmth of the drink in her face, flushing her skin.

'You are very beautiful, Miss Denniston. One of the most beautiful women I have ever seen.' His hand rested on hers now. She took a sip of the new drink and then finished it and when he removed the glass from her his arm brushed across her breasts in a way that felt wicked, her nipples hardening beneath the green silk.

'You should be in navy or gold. They would be your colours.'

'I tr-tried to tell my st-stepmother that.' She found that it was hard to form the words and there was a swimming sensation in her head. She wished Mr Rushworth would find her another drink, for she wanted more, and then he did.

'The last one, my dear, for I do not wish for you to fall asleep on me. No, indeed, I do not wish for that. Come, I want to show you something.'

Then they were in a long corridor all alone, curtains that went from ceiling to floor hiding them and he was kissing her, his tongue in her mouth and his body draped across her own.

Wrong. She tried to push him back.

'Too late for that, sweetheart, and you know it,' he returned and his hand came beneath her skirt and up into the space between her thighs, pushing in. Hurting hands and fingers... His mouth was across one breast now where he had snatched it from the silk, biting into flesh.

'The erotic suits you, with all your innocence and bounty and beauty.'

He moved against her then and groaned, his fingers stiffening in their place inside her and his face reddening as he stretched her.

The wine began to thump in her head as he finally removed his hand. The aches he had inflicted upon her echoed everywhere, the horror of it ascending, her acquiescence, his expectation, the flesh of her breast with its reddened nipple contrasting against green silk.

Leaning against the wall, she tried to find her balance, she was so speechless and shocked.

'We can continue this later, Miss Denniston, for you are now mine, a woman who was made for sex, for both the pain of it and for the pleasure.'

She shook her head. 'You will m-marry me?'

He laughed at that, a harsh ugly sound.

'Hardly. I meant that you shall be my mistress, for I cannot marry an unknown pauper from indeterminate stock with no family lineage whatsoever, no matter how beautiful.'

He reached forward then to pinch one nipple, hard.

'Put it away now before anyone sees you and do not say a word of this to anyone. And, Miss Denniston…' He smiled before continuing. 'I will teach you to kiss like the best of the courtesans, I promise you that, and when I have finished with you, you shall make a living like few others can.' His other hand cradled her chin, one finger following the line of her bottom lip. 'Open for me.'

She did, because she saw then in his face something dangerous and evil and it frightened her.

'That's better.'

One finger slipped inside and then a second one.

'Your mouth is made for sex, my dear, and we shall have plenty of it, I promise you that. I will one day be a baron and you shall be my mistress. Do you understand? It shall be our own delicious game, every hour that we want and all of the day and the night.'

He withdrew just as she thought she was about to gag, though one finger stayed against her lips.

'Shh. No talking. Tell no one and you and your family shall be safe.'

Then he was gone.

She began to shake so badly that she could barely make herself presentable again, her breast tucked away, her bodice pulled up and her skirts straightened. Swallowing hard, she was determined not to cry, not to create a fuss, not to draw attention to all that had just happened.

Had he deflowered her? Was that what he had just done?

She could hear the music though the curtains, feel the people there laughing and dancing, a world that she had been a part of before this had happened.

Now everything was different and he had threatened her with more should she speak of this. He had plied her with too much wine and brought her here with a purpose. It was not for love or conversation, but simply to hurt her with sex.

Among the fear and shame and dishonour, a small worm of anger rose, up and up until it was honed and refined and perfect.

She would not be ruined by this. She would not allow him the satisfaction of seeing her brought to heel. She nodded to herself and swallowed again. No, she would survive this and she would live.

A movement to one side behind the curtain ten moments later had her looking up.

Was Lord Rushworth back for more? Could she stop him? Unable to move, she froze solid and waited.

Her father drew back the curtain and appeared, his frown heavy when he saw her.

'Euphemia. We wondered where you had got to and Lucille said she had seen you coming this way half an hour ago with the dashing young Mr Rushworth, so after waiting for an appropriate time I have been sent to find you. My God, you are the belle of this ball and you should be thanking me for the green dress for it suits you as none of the others has. I have been fending off enquiries about you all night. We shall have a wealthy husband lined up in no time to save us all from penury and we will never have to worry again.'

These words fell across her in a torrent, giving her a little time to adjust.

No one else knew. No one understood what had just happened. Her father did not look at her as if she were ruined. No, he looked at her as though she were the key to a treasure undreamed of.

'The supper is about to be served and we do not wish to miss out on that now, do we, for Mr Rushworth is a man well worth pursuing. He holds large family lands in Cheshire, by all accounts, and is in line for the title.'

As her father led her back into the room in her lurid green dress with the too-low neckline and her flushed cheeks, she did not dare to glance around. If she saw Mr Rushworth in this setting, she knew she would go to pieces and she was adamant he would not destroy her.

She ate the supper and refused every other invitation afterwards to dance, staying with her father and stepmother until they pleaded tiredness and made for home. She could tell they were most disgruntled with her, but their annoyance was preferable to being anywhere near the man who had used her so abysmally.

Once in her room alone, she had torn off the green dress and thrown it into a corner, the bruised marks at her breast finally visible and the line of a scratch on one inner thigh a bright and angry red.

Ruined. Surviving. Furious. Ashamed.

So many emotions washed through her as she stood there in the cold, curtains drawn against the sleet which had started again and silence throughout the house.

She hated Mr Jeremy Rushworth and she hated herself for being so stupid. He had got her drunk and then he had effectively assaulted her. It was entirely her own fault. She deserved such abuse with the drink overcoming any sense and her hardened swollen nipples pointing outwards against the thin silk. She had asked for what she got.

Sitting on her bed, she put her head in her hands and allowed herself to cry, hot tears of humiliation and disgrace, any pride she'd had lost in the encounter with a man she had trusted.

Well, she would make sure she never trusted another one again. She swore that on the name of her mother.

Chapter Eight

Euphemia woke early, her fitful sleep and awful dreams leaving her with a heavy head and a nervous demeanour.

The same dream came every so often, but it had not been as real for years and years. Unbuttoning her nightgown, she looked down at the pale skin of her breasts and was relieved that no marks lay there. Just a dream. Mr Jeremy Rushworth was dead; she was safe. It could never happen again.

She dressed herself as soon as she got out of bed, her second-best day dress of mid-blue with the high-necked bodice exactly what she wanted to wear today.

She knew that Augustus Rushworth would not come and take her on the outing he had promised yesterday when the night was still young and hopeful. At the thought a sadness built for she would have loved to see the countryside outside of London and knew that her chance of ever going without August taking her was negligible.

August.

There it was again. The familiarity and the ease. She wished he would come.

Bobby had gone out so that the house was her own save for the cook in the kitchen who seemed to be constantly dozing; the food Mia had eaten last night at the ball was the first real meal she had eaten since Lucille and Susan had left four days ago.

But the silence comforted her.

Please do not let them return early, she found herself thinking. *Please keep them in Bath for the whole and full twelve days.*

She wrapped the golden dress in its calico shroud and tucked the shoes, gloves and fan into their boxes. The earrings she placed beside her necklace because she knew they were extremely old and precious and she did not want them to be misplaced.

Her clothes today were nothing like those she had worn last night, the aged blue velvet pulling at the seams, the fabric threadbare or patched in the places of the greatest use. Her second-best gown. She only had three.

She kept the cloak Augustus had sent out because it was another freezing day and if by some great chance he did come she would need something to ward away the chill.

If he came… She shook her head because she knew he wouldn't. He had been angry at her, she thought, and at the man who had stepped into his pathway. The words between them came back to her and she knew they had been speaking of Augustus's lost wife, Jane. Lost to death. Lost to infidelity. Lost to emptiness.

It was cold inside the house for there was not a fire lit downstairs. She was just wondering whether she should try to set one when there was a loud knock at the door, startling her.

Smoothing out her skirts and catching sight of her reflection in the mirror, she moved to the door and opened it.

Augustus stood there, larger than life, with a parasol opened above him. A gaudy parasol, too, in shades of red and yellow.

When he saw her looking, he smiled.

'I just purchased it from a street seller on the way here because the weather was so inclement. In India we used such things for the sun, but here it's for the constant rain. May I come in?'

'Yes, of course.' She fumbled with the handle as she went to close the door. 'I did not know whether to expect you or not, sir.'

The memory of her dream made it hard to look at him and she knew he noticed the awkwardness. She hated such unease between them, but could not seem to dispel it for this morning there was a new informality about him, a lightness that was appealing.

'I am sorry for last night's conversation with Sedgwick. As you have probably worked out, my marriage was not a happy one and my wife sought comfort in the arms of others. I blame myself as much as I blame her, for I was young and foolish. I proposed the instant

I met her and spent all the following years regretting it. We barely knew each other and when we did neither of us particularly liked what we discovered.'

Mia was glad he did not press all the blame on this lost wife, though she also had the impression that Augustus had been saddled right from the start with a woman who was unbalanced.

'How old was she when she died?'

'Twenty-six. She caught the cholera from a friend who had arrived in Bombay from the eastern coast.'

'Then perhaps it was lucky you were not there for I have read that it is a highly contagious disease.'

'It was.'

Others died, too, she thought then, others who had been close to him. Had they had children? She did not dare to ask.

Taking her hand in his own, he looked down at it. 'This is why I have no interest in being pressed into another union with a girl I barely know. I would also like to tell you how grateful I am for your help at the ball last night, but after Sedgwick's revelations if you wish to withdraw...'

'I don't.' The words fell from her mouth without thought and she found she did not want to take them back.

'I am not a saint, Euphemia.'

'And neither am I.'

'That I can't believe, but if you would allow me the grace of forgiveness I would still like to take you out and show you something of the countryside. There is also a house I think you will like...'

'A house?'

'My grandmother's estate, Stanthorpe Hall. It is a place I have not been to in years.'

'Who owns it?'

'I do. She left it to me because I used to spend a lot of time there with the others you met last night, too—Rupert, Bram, Tobias, young boys with a desire for freedom, I suppose—and, by heavens, did we make the most of it.'

'Will anyone else be there?'

'Only a few retainers—I made allowance for its security after I left England.'

How amazing, Mia thought, to own a house that had sat there unoccupied but staffed for ten years and then to return to it on a whim. The differences between them were beginning to mount up and she wished they would not.

'Did your other siblings receive land from her, too?' It was a dangerous question that was cutting close to home given her dream last night, but she could not help but ask.

'I had one brother who died four years after I left for India. But, no, Grandmère was a woman of strong opinion and as this estate was her own entirely she was able to give it to whomever she wanted.'

'She was French?'

'From Paris. My grandfather met her at a ball there and brought her home, though the marriage was fraught.

She missed her family and he was determined that she should stay in England no matter what, so by the time my father turned up they were largely estranged. I told you of the curse of the Rushworth men and how brides seem to bring out the worst in them?'

She liked his honesty and wondered about Augustus's explanation of his own marriage and the faults he confessed to having. Today he seemed to harbour no grudges about the difficulties at the ball and she was glad he still wanted to take her on a trip.

'Your house seems quiet. Are you alone here, Euphemia?'

'Well, almost. There is the elderly cook and the boy who does errands, but both are as pleased as I am with the change of circumstances in the house. I have seldom had time alone, you see, and I find it a great solace that will be hard to give up once my family comes back to London.'

'That cannot be safe. I will send a few servants over so that it is.'

'Please, no. I neither need nor want them. I lock the doors here and upstairs and there is nothing of value for anyone to take.'

'What of yourself?'

'Me?' She began to laugh. 'I will be thirty-one tomorrow so I doubt there will be a battery of marauders at my door, Mr Rushworth.'

'Tomorrow? It's your birthday?'

'It is.'

'Then we should celebrate it with a dinner at my town house.'

'Such a thing would cause a scandal, sir.'

'Only if it should become common knowledge, but who would need to know?'

This question was as shocking as his invitation to the ball and yet she could see why he had asked it. There was no one here who would question her attending such a dinner, but what of the servants at the Rushworth town house?

'The Rushworths have a small handful of loyal retainers who know how to keep a secret.'

It was as if he had read her mind and the startling possibility of actually saying yes became less outrageous. The ball had been one very public risk that she had taken and she would not have changed that for anything. Perhaps this was another more private one? If she did not take a chance now, she would be remorseful for ever, she knew that.

'I'm not sure…'

He smiled then and she had a sense of the boy he must once have been. The boy who had rescued all his friends from drowning, the boy who had left for India at nineteen and had not looked back.

'Give me a list of your favourite foods and I will have the cook make them.'

'That is quite an inducement, given the state of the kitchens here, Mr Rushworth.'

'So you will come?'

She nodded and felt a joy surge through her. *Take a chance, Euphemia,* she thought, *and live.*

She had always been afraid of touch, but with Augustus she found she no longer was. That thought was a revelation as he opened the gaudy parasol he'd recently purchased and shepherded her out to the conveyance.

It was a different carriage he showed her into today, a bigger, sleeker one with four greys standing at ease in front of it, their breaths white clouds in the air. Inside, plush velvet seating and warm woollen blankets banished the cold, and he unfolded one to place over her knees before taking the seat beside her.

'We will go by the Edgware Road. You will like the beauty of the countryside on the way.'

'Edgware is where your Grandmother's estate is?'

'It is. I used to go up there from school whenever I had the chance, for my father was not a man who kept an eye on me, so to speak, and it was not too far.'

'He lived here in London?'

'Generally, but he travelled a bit. We were not close, you understand.'

'And your grandfather?'

'He hardly ever left Amerleigh House. That's the country seat of the Rushworths.'

'But you went there in the school holidays?'

He shook his head. 'I went to the homes of my friends mostly, until the new term started.'

That piece of information made her pause.

'Well, at least you have them.' She said the words

before she had even digested the implications of what she just confessed and saw him watching her.

'Rupert Forsythe said that you vanished abruptly from society? He said there were rumours?'

'About me?'

She felt the blood drain from her face as horror kept her still.

'It is whispered you injured your leg running away from someone and screaming as you went. It was the talk of the town for a few weeks afterwards because when you fell there was quite a crowd to witness it, though no one ever knew the identity of the attacker. A big man, it was said, and rough with it.'

She turned to look out of the window, the rain heavier now so that all was blurry and far away, but inside the lantern burnt bright and the rug across her lap was warm.

She had seen Mr Jeremy Rushworth waiting for her in his carriage in Piccadilly two days after the Dashwoods' ball and when he had opened the door to speak with her, she had begun to run, as fast and as far as she was able. But he had sent his man after her, to rein her in, to bring her back, a man who would do his bidding exactly.

She had tripped on something as she looked back and broken her leg when she fell, and the protection of people who had come to help had saved her for he could hardly snatch her up then in the face of such notice. The last she had seen of the Rushworth carriage was it turning towards the Wellington Arch and speeding away.

'I left society of my own accord, Mr Rushworth. I chose to withdraw and forget.'

'And did you?'

'Never.'

He liked her vehemence because his had been exactly the same when Alice had died, a festering sore that had not healed.

He was pleased Euphemia kept her silence as to the reasons why she had left society, too, because it kept the day intact in a way a confession might not have. No, confessions broke everything apart, shattering the whole into pieces that could never be repaired. Jeremy's confessions had done that and so had his father's, unsolicited details that had almost killed him.

Leaning forward, Augustus thought carefully about what he might say next.

'When life is difficult a wise woman once told me you should take little steps, time after time, until the future looks like something you can manage.'

'Little steps?'

'A day in the country. A walk, if it stops raining, around a beautiful estate. We could look at the gardens.'

'Someone tends to them still after ten years of you being absent?'

'Money buys you many things, Euphemia, and I have a large amount of it.'

'Who was the wise woman, Mr Rushworth? The one you spoke of a moment ago?'

'A seer in Bombay who read the charts of time and

stars, and I found it heartening to believe that my life was going to become balanced again.'

She saw how his fingers strayed to the bracelet at his wrist, tracing the lines engraved in silver.

'Is that the language of India in the markings?'

He looked over at her and nodded. 'No, it's Marathi, the language of the state of Maharashtra.'

'You spoke it yesterday? To Mr Sedgwick?'

'I did.'

'India must have been a strange and different place.'

'I went at a time in my life when I needed something different. It was my grandfather who arranged it, though I only found that out the other day when he turned up at the town house in London. I was...ill, you see, and not inclined to notice much about my surroundings.'

He said this in a way that held other meanings, a secret, she thought, and was thrilled that he might give it into her safekeeping.

'But you recovered there and thrived.'

He laughed. 'I did, so there's the lesson. Allow life to take you where it will and you never know what might happen.'

A new intensity swirled around them, all humour suddenly gone. Mia knew he was talking about them, about this day.

He reached out for her hand, the gloves she wore a barrier preventing closer contact. 'Withdrawal can be difficult,' he said then, his voice quiet, a look in his eyes that drew her in, 'because you can get stuck there.'

Peeling off her glove, Augustus drew a line with his

finger on the inside of her palm, the touch making her breathe in deeply.

'I did the same once. I found a solace in isolation for a while and then it became a prison. The thing is, Miss Denniston…' There was a note of hope in the formality of his speech. 'The thing is, perhaps this pact of ours is a chance for both of us to find a life that is easier. I want to get to know you. I want to know what it is like to hold you close.'

His eyes burnt into her own, but he had told her that he did not want another bride or anything permanent. So where did that leave them?

'We could go slowly.'

More words to add to the equation. Slowly enough to heal her? Slowly enough to survive? He would not try to rip her clothes from her breast at a ball or have his men chase her across a busy street shouting obscenities as she fled from such vitriol…

She made herself stop. Augustus Rushworth was not his brother and she was not the young girl she had once been either. Unless she took a chance here and now, she would be consigned to loneliness for ever. He was not rushing her. He would let her go at her pace, slowly, gently and without force.

Her fingers closed around his in answer, a small caress as the carriage passed by some of the busiest streets of London.

She had not snatched her hand away. He swallowed because such an acquiescence was so unexpected.

His wife Jane had been a loud and shallow woman, a girl who had hidden such traits carefully on their first meetings and one who had wooed him using her body with an artful deceit.

Euphemia was nothing like that. Her clothes were prim and her bearing was careful, all traits that hid the clever and kind and honest woman beneath.

But there were other parts of Euphemia which he now thought of, too—her curves, her softness, the way she moved and spoke and laughed. She was sensual in a way other women never were, unaware of and oblivious to all the glances that turned her way as she had walked through the ballroom in her golden dress.

The thump of need he felt to bring her closer was constant and wearisome, but he had promised he would not rush her and he meant to stand by such a pledge.

He was not inexperienced, for after Jane died he had known other women intimately. In private, of course, and without fanfare. He was not like Jeremy with his constant wanderings and his never-ending trumpeting of physical victory over this woman or that one.

No, he'd been careful with his distance, always generous but never giving them much of himself, preferring instead a detachment that would allow him escape.

But from that very first second of seeing Euphemia's upturned face on the dock at the Frost Fair, Augustus had felt something he never had before.

A desperate longing to know her.

These words worried him because he had promised himself, after Alice, never again to get attached to anyone.

Euphemia moved now, facing him, her blue eyes regarding him with a look that held no pretence at all.

'Once, a long time ago, a man wanted more from me than I wished to give him.'

'Was he the one who hurt you?'

She didn't answer, but there was a darkness in her glance that told him that it was.

Unlacing their hands, he slipped a ring off his little finger.

'Rubies symbolise energy, passion and power.' He closed her hand around the jewel. 'The power to leave the past behind if you are willing to.'

'I couldn't accept this…'

He stopped her simply by raising his hand.

'Someone gave it to me when I needed it, but now I don't, so when you have finished with its magic you can pass it on, too. The Hindus believe that karma is not fate and that each of us acts with a conditioned free will to create our own destiny. They also believe that no other person can determine your aspect of self, even though they might try to.'

'You are saying it is me who is in charge of myself?'

'I am.'

She leant forward at that and brushed her lips across his cheek, like a whisper or a shadow, and he was astonished. He could see she was shocked as well, an action that had probably surprised her as much as it had him.

She smelt like springtime and promise.

* * *

God, what had she done? For all the years since the Dashwoods' ball she had not touched another person in such a way, her reticence for any close contact often remarked upon by her sister and her stepmother.

Yet when he'd reached over to place the ring in her hand she had felt no alarm at all and when he had told her of her right to determine herself, something had clicked inside of her.

Augustus Rushworth was not manipulative, deceitful or hurtful. He was sensual and kind and thoughtful, and he had been hurt, too, the webbed map of scars easily discernible across the back of his hand.

Here in the carriage hurtling north with the rain all around them, Mia felt alive in a way she never had before, the air charged with a power that was impossible not to notice.

Perhaps the ring did hold the magic of which he spoke, a healing power and a passion, because under her shock she felt other things moving, spiralling across her body, thawing her frozen heart. She knew she was not beautiful and yet he seemed to find her so. He listened to her opinions with interest and when she had told him how old she was he had replied that he thought she looked much younger.

He was not trying to change her or make her different. He liked her just as she was.

And here, close to him inside the carriage, she finally felt that perhaps she was enough.

She knew the ring would be too big on her finger so

she unclasped her silver chain necklace and threaded it through, liking the heavy warmth of it against her breast when she tucked it down inside her bodice.

She thought she saw him smile as she did so.

When they arrived he helped her out, the small courtesy of another's touch leading her to wonder what might happen next between them.

Stanthorpe Hall was exquisite, a property of cream stone baked pale in the thin light of an English February. It was also far bigger than she had expected, two triple-storeyed wings jutting out from the central façade.

'My grandmother was from one of the great land-owning families of France. She used this place as an escape from Amerleigh House.'

'A sanctuary?'

He nodded and tightened his grip on her hand.

'I need to make myself known to the servants and then we can be alone.'

Alone.

The word reverberated through her. Alone to do what?

She suddenly imagined them in a large room with gauzy curtains and a bed near a blazing fire. She saw them bare-skinned and close on the counterpane, her hair falling around them, blonde against dark as he moved across her, his arms powerful, the scar on her lower leg easily visible.

Shocked, she felt her heartbeat quicken.

Would she do it? Would she allow him all she was

imagining in this pale stone house far from London? She who had been celibate all of her life save for that one groping, hurting time when she had been intoxicated at the Dashwoods' ball and lost her innocence?

Her thirty-first birthday was tomorrow and in the fourteen years since she had left society she had been frightened, yet here was some other pathway, an interlude far from London with no strings attached.

She felt a loosening inside her and a rising heat. Her eyes took in all the windows visible on the second floor. Which bedroom would they retire to? Would the door be locked and the curtains drawn?

So many questions without answers. Her insides drew back into a tight ball of hope.

'I have asked for a luncheon to be set out, Euphemia.' Augustus's words were so far from all she had been thinking that for a moment she was confused. 'I thought you might be hungry and we could eat before we take a look around the place.'

He was not going to whisk her off upstairs and undress her?

He would feed her first.

The relief was overwhelming.

'The estate runs a farm which provides it with all manner of provisions and the cheese here is especially well known locally.'

Augustus grimaced as he listened to the run of words. All he wanted to do was to take down her golden hair and see her pale-skinned curves in the soft bare light of day.

He could feel himself hardening at the sheer thought of it and pulled his cloak in more tightly.

Euphemia had been badly frightened by someone when she was younger so she could hardly be wanting anything like the scenario rolling around in his mind.

Breathing out, he took his hand from the small of her back, the shape of her bottom against wool as distracting as hell. She was so beautifully made, that was the problem, the curves because of her small frame even more noticeable. She was a woman who was enticing without meaning to be, a reluctant siren who had no idea of what she was doing to him.

He doubted he'd be able to eat at all given he was so on edge and here he was deliberating on the properties of the estate's cheese.

It was her blue eyes, he decided then, and her dimples. Her voice was a big part of it, too, and the tumbling honey-blonde length of her hair.

He'd promised himself he would be more careful in choosing another companion after the fiasco of his hasty marriage to Jane, yet here, on only his second outing with Euphemia Denniston, he was trying to work out all the ways he could get her into his bed, thus enabling him to get to know her body intimately.

And her mind.

That part of the equation worried him more than the first because every conversation they had had left her shrouded in more and more mystery.

'You run a home farm on the estate, then?' Her question came through the fog and he struggled to make sense of the context.

'The cheese,' she continued when he didn't speak.

'Oh, indeed. My grandmother was quite wise. Her own father was a landowner in Normandy and she had enjoyed the detail of it. When she died she made certain to tell me all the things she wanted kept in place.'

'Even though you were young?'

'Well, I always liked the feel of the land and the way the seasons changed it, and as she had left the estate to me I felt a certain responsibility to make certain her wishes were honoured. It's part of the reason I want to settle in the countryside.'

'But you would not wish to come here?'

'It's a beautiful estate, but it's complete in its way. If I did decide to live here, there are things I would change.'

'And what of your grandfather and his wishes for your family?'

'He would have me settled at Amerleigh House with all the rigid rules that living under his roof entails and the place would be a trap.'

'You have a wealth of options, though, and in that you are lucky for many people do not have such a luxury of choice.'

Her blue gaze did not falter.

'Like you do not?' He had to ask.

'My father burnt his bridges with his family years before I was born, but I would have liked to have people around me who I could have known.'

'Family is not always as tidy as that, Euphemia. Most can only disappoint you.' He thought of his brother and his father, and his grandfather to a lesser extent.

'But at least you shared the same bloodlines so you had that in common.'

'Unlike your stepmother and stepsister?'

She nodded.

'They are not bad people, but if I was not there they would barely notice save for the help that I give them. A family should be more than that, I think.'

August experienced an ache unlike anything he'd ever known. He'd managed his family's betrayals by beginning a new life in India far away from them all, but she had been unable to do that. He'd heard the stories of her unexpected departure from society and had seen the way she had been treated almost as a nuisance by her stepmother, all the woman's attention settled on the younger daughter. He'd noticed how she'd tried to appear invisible, too, only the ghost of herself left inside her shell. Her grief had been a different version of his own, more prolonged and less brutal perhaps, but it had also been largely immured in a loneliness that he could not imagine.

And here she was, allowing her stepfamily a forgiveness that was both generous and unspeakably poignant, the navy cloak contrasting with the wisps of blonde hair blowing around her face in the wind.

Beautiful and strong.

She was not flighty or unreliable. What she promised was what he had been given and when there were problems she had tried to explain them to him.

It was what had been missing from his family, this loyalty and honour, this sense of trust that was dependable and steadfast.

The servants had come out to meet them, people he remembered from childhood, their smiles warm, and after greeting them he shepherded Euphemia up the front steps and into the house proper.

The familiar smells of the place made him relax. The polish used on the floor was one he remembered well, as were the candles burning on the table by the wall. His grandmother had had a passion for scented herbs and had filled the wax with them in all the rooms of her house. Today, the smell of lemon verbena wafted in the air.

In the springtime there would be large bunches of flowers everywhere and in the summer it would be the turn of the roses to take over the house. There were stands of rose bushes behind the house, in all colours and shapes.

He'd had a happy time here when he was young, an interlude from the violence and hostility of his family residing at Amerleigh though he had told Euphemia he had largely stayed away from Cheshire, that was not quite true. There had been times when he had been summoned there.

Claudia Rushworth had not chosen her husband's family portraits to be hung on the walls at Stanthorpe. Rather, a series of her French relatives looked down on him from all angles, happier prosperous people who appeared respectable and decent.

Grandmère had always spoken in French to him and the sound of the language came back, the ditties and the songs that were so much a part of his early years. He remembered coming here to Stanthorpe Hall from Amerleigh House, damaged and frightened, before being shipped off to India on the first available boat.

It was a woman's house, Mia thought, full of the touches of someone who enjoyed colour, for every wall was of a different hue, giving the place the look and style of a foreign land.

The paintings were interesting as well, a full range of portraits on the stairwell as they walked into a salon bordered by windows which led out on to a garden. A small table was set up before a blazing fire, the crockery of blue and white very un-English-looking.

On the wall was a portrait of a much younger Augustus Rushworth. He stood alone before a fountain, a dog beside him.

When he saw where she was looking he smiled. 'That was a portrait my grandmother commissioned from a local painter. The dog was one of her own and whenever I was here he shadowed me.'

'What was his name?'

'Soldat. Soldier. He was like a guard and accompanied me everywhere.'

'You sound as though you liked it here.'

'I did.'

He never mentioned his family much, save with distaste, she thought then. Not even once had he spoken at length about his brother or his father.

'I was often here at Easter. There is a tree somewhere around, probably stored in the attic, with all the eggs we blew and painted on each successive year. When Grandmère died and left her estate to me it created friction because my father thought it should have come straight to him. My brother was just as unhappy.'

'But she wanted you to have it?'

'I think she imagined I was the safer bet for both its prosperity and its longevity and as it was her own personal property they could do nothing about her bequest.'

An interesting observation, she thought. His grandmother had trusted him more than the others and Mia could well understand why.

'I often wonder if my father's parents could still be alive somewhere; I know my mother's parents died early.'

'Do you have any idea where your grandparents hailed from?'

'York, I think. I remember asking Papa once and he said they would want nothing at all to do with us and that York was a long way away so it was better to just forget about them.'

'Would you like me to send someone up there to look? It might garner some information, at least.'

The very idea had her standing still. 'I am not sure…'

'What more could you lose than you have already, Euphemia, by knowing?'

'If they declined to want to contact me and I knew they were alive, I think it would be harder still. You cannot understand what it is like to have no one in the world who is related to you.'

'It sounds rather attractive from where I sit.'

Without meaning to she began to laugh. 'Then maybe I am not as badly off as I always thought, Mr Rushworth.'

'August.' His voice was quiet as she walked to the window to look out on to the garden as well as to be nearer to him.

She felt him behind her, close, the heat of him and the strength. She could never remember being so easy in anyone's company before, though an edge of panic that took her breath away was a worry. It was as though she stood on the top of a cliff ready to jump off, and whether it was into deep blue water or jagged sharp rocks she had yet to find out.

Ever since the Dashwoods' ball she had been careful, every pathway considered, each outing pondered and deliberated on. But here in this room with the light streaming through the glass doors and the winter garden outside she felt released and safe. A sanctuary far from London, far from Lucille and Susan, far from anyone or anything she had known.

If this house were mine I would never leave it, she found herself thinking. *I should stay here for ever and tend to the plants and watch the trees and the hills and the sky.*

Chapter Nine

The thought that his grandmother would have liked Euphemia Denniston came out of nowhere, but standing there outlined before the garden she looked so much a part of Stanthorpe Hall that August was astonished.

Perhaps belonging was not just tied up with people, but with places, too. Her London address on Bolton Street was dark and threadbare, a place of toil and emptiness, a house that gave no impression at all of being a home. She had no true family, no relatives and no friends; her world was a lonely one that demanded endurance to survive it. Yet she had survived with braveness, perseverance and honesty.

When he did not speak she turned towards him, a question in her bright blue eyes.

'I like watching you.' His explanation had her blushing, the red staining pale cheeks and making her eyes appear even brighter.

'Then you are the first person who ever has, August.'

She had called him by his Christian name which was another first.

'You look happy.'

'I think I am. It's calm here and quiet. Always in London there is noise, but here...'

'Here the world stops.'

She smiled. 'It does. And the air is so clear I can see all the way to the trees in the distance.'

'When I was young I used to pretend they were the forests of Camelot surrounding my castle and I was Arthur.'

'Not Lancelot?'

'No, a king ruled them all and I liked the idea of that.'

'I wish I'd known you then, for the freedom you speak of sounds unbelievably wonderful.'

'Where did you live when you were young?'

'Anywhere and everywhere in the middle of London with my father. He did not want to settle and so there were a number of lodgings, some better than others.'

'How old were you when he met your stepmother?'

'Fourteen. An age that is difficult for girls, I think, and Lucille did not particularly want a stepdaughter, especially a sullen one like I was.'

'When did you come out in society then?'

'At seventeen, which was early, and I was too young to cope.'

'With suitors?'

She shook her head hard. 'I never had any of those and I left before I did.'

The secrets were back, but some truths were there,

too, hidden among the words. Why had she not coped in society and when had the difficult young girl turned into this careful and controlled one?

Tobias had said Euphemia Denniston had been surrounded by suitors and Bram had made a point of telling him of her success when she had been brought out.

Something had happened to her, something that was not known in society.

The man who had hurt her surfaced, the one she had told him of when she had stated that she did not like to be kissed. The story of her being attacked in Piccadilly was also a part of it—perhaps that was why she limped sometimes.

He knew what happened to women who had been abused because of his brother's exploits, a man without morals or feelings. Could this have happened to Euphemia?

He stepped forward and stood beside her, but he did not touch her.

'I would never hurt you.'

'I know, you've already said.'

Her hand came out then and took his.

'If you give me time…'

'As much as you need.'

'Thank you.'

The wind blew in against the glass, the brown shrubs of his grandmother's garden waving in the breeze, and further off in the distance the purple clouds gathered. The sun would not be out for much longer.

He wished it might snow so much that they were cut

off, the roads impassable, the temperatures so cold that no one could venture forth. It would be a way of keeping her here with him, for a while at least.

'Once when I was young my father told me of the cold-loving, bow-wielding Ullr, a Norwegian god who would glide around the world and cover the land with snow. I think he is on his way.'

August nodded. She had noticed the clouds, too.

'Your father was well read?'

'He was an academic and he liked the legends of old times the most because it allowed him to live in the past.'

'He found the present difficult, then?'

'He did, although strong drink helped him to cope.'

Another clue, a further sadness.

'People have their buttresses, I suppose. When I was in India, travel was mine.'

'Because it let you escape?'

'Yes.' But it was not the full truth at all. If he'd wanted to escape he would have taken their daughter with him, to safety. Instead he had left her there in the company of a mother who was either depressed or elated, and the cholera had come from the east, invited in with guests.

The linkage of their hands was like a safe harbour and he wished he could take Euphemia in his arms and kiss her, to know the taste of her and the softness. He wanted this so much he could barely breathe.

For the first time ever she was not afraid of a man. She wanted to keep Augustus beside her, here in this house of peace and quietness. Just the two of them, far from London and from her life there.

A further thought surfaced. He had asked her last night at the ball to spend the night with him and he had also said he wanted to get to know her better and to hold her close. Not as a wife, because she knew he did not offer that, but as a lover.

A lover?

For once the term failed to hold the fear it had always engendered and she saw in the closeness of intimacy an escape.

He would go carefully, he had promised that. He would not rush her, either.

But how could she show him she wanted more than just holding hands? How could she make him see that her fear of him was changing into something different?

She could not tell him of her foolishness with his brother either, the way she had allowed him to take her from the room and get her drunk, the way he had touched her, ruined her…

She had no idea what to do next.

A knock at the door had them both turning as he dropped her hand and an older, plump woman came in.

'We have luncheon prepared, sir. Will you have it in here?'

'Thank you, Mrs Creighton. That would be lovely.'

Behind her, others streamed in with plates and utensils and large bowls of steaming food in their hands.

After a moment or two of setting it all out, the older woman waited until the other servants left before turning to Augustus.

'I hope you enjoy lunch, Mr Rushworth. If there is anything else you require, you only need to ring.'

'I am sure everything will be just fine.'

Then it was just them, no attending servants or listening ears. Mia realised then that she was starving and walked forward to lift the covers off roast chicken and vegetables and freshly baked bread. Other smaller dishes sat there, too, a fine lunch of country fare, including a pie that looked like it contained apple with a small jug of thick cream beside it.

There were biscuits, too, and fruit and marzipan shapes rolled in sugar.

She could not remember a time when she had been offered this much food at one meal save for the supper at the Barretts' ball last night. It seemed incredible that the staff here should have whipped up such a feast because, if she had her facts right, Augustus had not been here for ten years.

There was an ease in his house and company, the struggle of the last years far from this luxury. But it was not just about that. Augustus made her feel as if she might relax her vigilance and live and that was worth more than she could have ever said.

He helped her into a seat and took the one opposite on the small table.

'Does anything take your fancy?' he asked, picking up the serving spoons and waiting for her instructions.

When she pointed at the chicken, vegetables and bread, he gave her a generous helping of them all and then served himself the same meal.

'The cook has recently come back from London where she has worked in some of the most discerning kitchens in the land.'

'Then you were lucky to get her for this is delicious.'

'Her family is from these parts and she always said she would return if I did.'

'So they knew you were coming?'

'Yes. I sent word last year and the place was readied. It's the only home I have at the moment.'

'And one of the most beautiful houses in England, too, I think.'

'You have been out of London for no more than half a day. There are many more grand estates than this one.'

'But there is something here, isn't there? A peace and a stillness?'

'My grandmother always thought there was. She said Amerleigh House was full of importance and power, but that Stanthorpe Hall held harmony.'

'She was right.'

'Did your father never travel away from London?'

'He did, but only for short spells. He went off on his own quite often, but he always left me behind.'

'At school?'

'No. I was not enrolled anywhere, but he had a good library and I used it until Lucille sold off most of the books.'

'That must have been hard.'

'Well, I had read them all and she gave me a home, so I was luckier than most.'

Her smile was half-hearted.

'After lunch I will show you the library here. I am sure you will be impressed.'

'Did your wife read much?'

'Never. She was happiest in the company of many friends, and the louder the better.' He looked around. 'Jane would have found this place deathly quiet. She would have insisted we return to London immediately to enjoy the whirlwind of the *ton*.'

His daughter, on the other hand, would have sat here for ever. He'd had books sent out from England for her to read, story books with pictures so she might imagine what life was like here and want to visit one day.

He reached forward and took Euphemia's hand because he needed the warmth of her touch and he did not wish to be lost in the past today.

'My wife and I were ill suited right from the start. I'd arrived in India with injuries and she was kind. Then.'

It was as much as he wanted to say.

'Your hand?'

'And my arm. I'd been in a fight and had lost badly.'

'So India was an escape of sorts?'

'It was. But in the end I found a peace there and a spirituality that suited me.'

'Yet you came back?'

He frowned. 'Do you ever think that life might be lived in chapters? You close one chapter and open another and for a while you look back, but then your head turns to the front and then that is all you want to see.'

'I like that. It feels restorative.'

'Perhaps this is a new chapter, then. Here, for us? The start of turning around and looking forward.'

'Not back?'

He brought her hand to his lips and kissed each finger.

'You are beautiful, Euphemia, and clever, and you have your whole life in front of you.'

'I had not thought so before I saw you on the docks at the Frost Fair.'

'But now...'

She watched as he stood and came around behind her, pulling her up to him, his eyes dark, the closeness astonishing. A closeness not like in a waltz, but filled with other things. She felt out of her depth yet spellbound.

One finger gently traced the line of her cheek and stayed there, careful and searching, the shape of his body under fine clothing felt with such nearness. She moved unbidden into the heated curve of him and into the touch of his hand, a touch that asked of her things she was not sure she could give.

But he did not hurry her. As the seconds passed a thrall unlike anything she had known began to build because maybe it was possible to feel the things that other women did, to stay here in his arms and wish for more.

She felt his lips against her temple, small intimacies that ignited an appetite she had half known in her dreams, slipping across sense and enveloping it.

She wanted to be here, near him, the slow urge of movement inside her growing. Her grip tightened on his arm, to stall the falling, to find an anchor, to keep him there with her wordless powerful need, the dream tethers loosened into the shock of the real.

Nothing mattered save for him and she was lost in this magic.

'Mia?'

His voice.

She opened her eyes and looked at him.

'May I kiss you?'

Her throat tightened, not with tears but with emotion. He sought her permission and she gave it, in a small nod and a quiet promise.

She felt him turn her head as he leaned down and then his mouth covered hers, a soft and gentle touch, light with care.

There was no reminder of that night at the ball years ago. Her breath settled, no spike of panic ensuing, no broken fear or barb of terror. Just him and her, here in a house smelling of scented lemon candles and firelight, here in a room where she was safe and sheltered and valued.

He pulled away and she watched him, saying things with her eyes that were impossible with words, allowing him more.

'You are beautiful.'

His breath tickled one cheek as he said this, his gaze focused on her, and for the first time in her life she thought that perhaps she was beautiful. To him.

When he kissed her again, shivers chased each other across her skin and this time she kissed him back, opening her mouth to his and feeling his promise. He did not hurry or hurt her. He came in softly and offered himself and it was this more than anything that made her lace her fingers around the back of his neck and pull him closer, this time with the intent of finding an ancient truth, the one that came from hope and faith.

His body heard hers for he deepened the kiss, the breath between them shared, life combined in seconds and in minutes.

He was hard and large and unbreakable, a man whose past had not ruined him, a man who could still find the softness under hurt. Mia wanted to rise up with him into the place that held no notion of time or loss, the place that simply belonged to the two of them.

Her head tipped and she gave him back what he was giving her, the gentle calmness charged now with hunger. It was just as the romances she read from Lackington's under candlelight promised, the ones she enjoyed deep in the night when she could savour them without interruption.

Like a chasm without limit, falling and falling into space, the knowledge of change and discovery, the delight as much a part of it as the more unexpected fever, all control disappeared as excitement took over. He kissed her as if she were priceless and irreplaceable, as if she were beyond monetary worth. He kissed her with his heart and his soul, without compromise or limits or judgement.

He marked her with this ardour not in bruises or scratches, but in the soft air of breath and worship. She liked the taste of him and the feel and when he finished the kiss and drew her in she went, her head fitting under his neck and his arms about her.

Like a puzzle that had found the final piece and was now complete.

'I have dreamed of kissing you, Euphemia, ever since I first met you.'

'I hope it was not a disappointment or—'

But he stopped her by a quick kiss.

'It wasn't.'

His arms lay around her back, the warmth of him startling.

'I did not know kissing could be like that.'

'Usually it isn't, believe me.'

She began to smile and he must have felt it because he tipped back, his eyebrows raised.

'Are you laughing at me, Miss Denniston? Do you not take what I say as the truth?'

'I have not kissed anyone before so I have no idea, Mr Rushworth.' She did not count the attack at the Dashwoods' ball because that had not been a kiss, but an assault, and it was only now that she knew the difference.

'That is a defence that I can accept as exemplary and one I am glad of.'

Humour threaded through his words and just the feel of him made her blood sing, a happiness coursing through her that was so unfamiliar it made her dizzy. Like a normal girl, like a woman who was not impaired. Perhaps it was possible to go from that to this after all.

It just took courage and a man who was prepared to give her time.

She knew it could not be for ever, but this now was enough.

Outside, the sun broke again through the clouds, fleeing across the sky.

'Show me the gardens. Give me a tour before it rains for I would like to see them.'

'Very well. I am presuming you have finished eating?'

'I have. I could not eat another thing, but it was all delicious. Your cook is a magician.'

'My staff generally stays with me. I have not had one who has up and left.'

'Then I am glad to hear of it for that tells me a lot about your character.'

'Such as…?'

He was teasing her and she knew it but such banter made her smile.

'You are loyal and kind and a man not prone to tantrums.'

'I hope not.'

'You expect loyalty and get it because you are loyal in return.'

His finger ran across the bridge of her nose.

'You sound like a woman with a vast experience of servants.'

'Not servants, but servitude. I know what wins over those who work for others and what does not.'

'Your stepmother obviously had trouble?'

'Constantly. She treats people without consideration or compassion.'

'Like my father and brother. They were the masters of no humanity.'

Euphemia waited for the panic which usually came from any surprise mention of the late Mr Rushworth, but it did not arrive. Another change.

'But come, I will show you the gardens after we find your cloak and hat because you will need such things to keep at least a little warm.'

In India the weather was either very hot or moderately hot and the skies apart from in the rainy season were always an endless and changeless blue. At first he had enjoyed the tropics, but as time went on he had found himself longing for the cleansing sound of rain and the changing of the seasons.

So the promise of snow was not wished away at all, but welcomed, for he loved how the world quietened under its presence as it drew itself in.

With Euphemia by his side a few moments later and in warmer clothes, they plodded through the puddles on the lawns to one side of the gardens and then he found the path that ran down the middle of it.

'When my grandmother was alive she was always here, tending and pruning and collecting the bounty. My grandfather said she had the hands of a servant and I think she saw that as a compliment.'

'She sounds like a fascinating woman.'

'She was.'

He saw her looking around, taking in the shapes and the levels of it all that were apparent even now before spring had come and when the plants lay dormant and waiting.

He wanted to take her in his arms again and resume the kiss that they had started over lunch, but all the windows of the house overlooked them here and anyone might see so he stood back. She turned just as he did, her bright blue eyes locked upon him.

'I told you once that I did not like to be kissed, but I think that has changed now.'

Her honesty astounded him.

'So you are saying you would like me to kiss you again?'

'I know our pact did not stretch to such a thing and I would not expect more, but I liked it and after so many years of being afraid it is nice not to be.'

His heart thumped in his chest and he led her over to a covered walkway out of the wind and out of sight, for the trellis on its walls created a private space and one easily big enough for them both.

When they were there he felt her come to him willingly, but then everything changed.

Before, his kiss had been tentative and careful, an intimacy given with the knowledge of her fear so he had held back and bridled his passion. But now he simply let go.

His mouth was heat and longing, the touch of a man who had known the world and known women. He was no longer cautious, the latent power once harnessed was now unleashed. It should have frightened her, this difference, but it didn't. Instead it made her bolder and more daring, a woman who would be thirty-one tomorrow and who was finally being kissed properly. Everything else that had come before fell away and she could think of nothing save his mouth opening on to hers with a fierce intimacy and a practised expertise.

A rising wave of sensation came across her, knifing through her body, making her hot and hungry for more. She brought her hands to his head and pulled him in, wanting everything he offered and more. His tongue tangled with hers, the breath between them shared, and there was a new urgency, a dark magic that held no limit.

It was just them in this world for nothing and no one else existed, her body drawing itself into a crescendo, a pitch of need, and then beaching into the languid, waves of relief rushing through her as she clung to him without breath, feeling the wonder.

He held her tight, his mouth gone and his touch quieter now, waiting, allowing the silence. Her nails dug into the fabric of his jacket, her hands shaking with the effort of reaching for a place she had never been before, a place between this world and the next.

'Thank you.' She said this finally when she could speak again and he held her as if she were something infinitely precious. She felt no sense of embarrassment or awkwardness for his eyes watched her as though she were wonderful.

'I will never walk this garden again without thinking of this moment, Euphemia, because reincarnation is a key belief within Hinduism. In Hinduism, all life goes through birth, life, death and rebirth and this is known as the cycle of samsara.'

'Samsara. A beautiful word.'

'And I think this is yours.'

'But there is more?'

She asked this because her body felt ready to know all the secrets of what she'd never had and because if she lost this chance here with him she might never know it again.

'Much more.'

His voice had deepened as he gave her his reply and an intensity sat between them, a force that connected them and this moment of rebirth.

'Show me.'

He shook his head as she reached for him.

'Not here.'

His eyes took in the front façade of the house as she saw him thinking and then he took her hand.

'Come.'

Chapter Ten

They walked away from the house, down another hidden path and through a copse of trees until there in front of them stood a cottage.

'Wait here.'

He went to the door and tried it, but it was locked. Then he strode around to the back of the house and a moment later the same door opened from inside and he was there.

'How did you get in?'

'The same way I used to when I was younger. There's a catch on the back window that's loose.'

He picked her up then in his arms and walked across the threshold, like a groom might have done with his new bride.

Inside, it was far prettier than she had expected, a pale white and cream decor so very different from the heavier colours of the house.

A large bed sat in the middle of the room, a net hung down around it from wooden slats.

'Is it an Indian style?' She had never seen anything like it.

'No. French. My grandmother's family again.'

It was much warmer inside than she would have expected and Mia guessed that came from the thickness of the walls and the smallness of the windows.

'Like a sanctuary.' She wondered if he had used it often as a youth growing up.

'Exactly.'

He crossed to the bed and knotted the nets to one side. A bed with a light yellow and blue quilt came into view, a stack of pillows resting against a headboard of cream.

Their place. She took in a breath as she saw it, for the dark heat of him in here was larger somehow and much more immediate.

'You are sure?'

She knew vaguely of what he asked, this permission, this consent to do with her just as a thousand lovers had done over the course of time. To consume and to take, to be one with each other through the coming together of their bodies. She had seen the pictures in her father's books after all, the ancient statues, the crude drawings, the penned caricatures of street prostitutes and great ladies lying prostrate on their beds of lust.

Was this her bed of lust? What would she know after an hour or two or a whole night of loving? Would it be like the kiss, a magical unexpected delight, or were there other things at play?

When he saw her frown he walked over to her and stopped there without touching.

'Are you a virgin, Euphemia?'

'Yes.'

'Hell, I thought...' He stopped and swallowed.

'He did not rape me, the man I told you of, but he hurt me and I deserved it.'

'Why?'

'Because I was intoxicated. Because I had not enough sense to say no more. Because I took drink after drink without a care. Because I left a room full of others and was alone with him.'

'Did he give you the drinks? Did he know you were an innocent, young and unprotected?'

'Yes.'

'Then it was his fault. He led you into the chaos. You were seventeen so how could you have known otherwise and there are men like that—'

He stopped abruptly.

'It's why you drink the orange cordial?'

'Yes.'

'One glass of wine can relax you. It's not always a bad thing.'

His hand came up and pulled at the fastenings of the cloak he had brought her and she did not stop him. When he placed the garment over a nearby chair she did not move away either. Her breasts felt full under her old day dress and a feeling between her legs began to grow.

She wanted to be naked and lying in the half-light on the netted bed with its rich counterpane beneath

her. She wanted his hands on her and his lips, too, she
wanted him to be inside her, warm and hidden, dark
and hard.

She did not say these things, though, because they
were scandalous, but this was what she thought. The
ripe bounty of her flesh pressed outward as though asking for his ministrations.

He lifted her hat off easily, discarding it on the table
near the bed. Then he started on her hair, each pin dis-
mantling her armour until it fell loose down her back
and over her shoulders, a curling thick mass of blonde.

'I wondered what the colour of your hair would be
when I first met you and this is exactly what I imagined.'

She did not speak because to do so might break the
spell, might stop him, might allow for hesitation, but
she frowned as he stepped away and found in a small
cupboard a bottle of wine and two glasses.

'Not to get drunk on, but to relax with. I promise it
will help.'

She took the glass and went to drink it quickly, but
he slowed her down by placing a finger on the rim.

'A little at a time is best, Euphemia, and this is strong
wine.'

It was far better taken in small doses and she enjoyed
the taste. She would trust him with these instructions
just as she would trust him with her body.

When they had finished, he took the glasses and
placed them on the table with all her hairpins and hat,

then he kissed her, the taste between them a new sensation, a taste of wine and man and lust.

This kiss was different again from the others he had given her. There was a certainty there now and a promise, his mouth falling lower to her neck and then to the folds at the edge of her dress where he sucked at the skin until she burned with it, a map of loving, each part as glorious as the last one.

She had no idea what he might do next, but in here anything was permissible and he knew it.

She wished she might take more wine, but he did not offer. She wished he would undress her quickly and finish it so that the worry might be over, but he did not do that either.

Rather he tarried, his fingers pulling at the stays on her bodice, loosening them slowly until the fabric fell forward and free, only her petticoat shielding her.

His fingers dipped underneath lawn, the swell of her breast in his hand now, filling it. She looked at him, willing him to say something, but he only smiled.

Her breathing changed, heavier and faster, and she could feel the beat of her heart through her skin and knew that he did, too.

He pulled the thin lawn away and her bodice with it so that she stood before him clothed only from the waist down.

'Lord, help me.'

The words cut through the air and she squared her shoulders and looked at him.

'You are made like one of the ancient goddesses who has just escaped from Greece and is mine to savour.'

His tongue traced a line from her neck downwards and his mouth came across one nipple, taking it and sucking. The moist heat inside her moved and a sound was ripped from her that spoke of desire, low and carnal, untranslatable. He suckled at her as a child might, finding her centre, the glorious pain of it echoing inside.

Not a child, then, but a man, this man, hard and ready, strong and true. When he looked up and took his mouth away from her his mouth was wet and so was her breast.

Nothing was left as it had been, pristine, white and unmarked. Her nipple stood up like a cherry, hard and rigid, proclaiming need. He rolled it between his fingers and looked at her.

'I will be gentle.'

'I know.'

'But I am not sure if I can stop should you allow me more.' His glance fell down and she saw the outline of his sex straining at his breeches.

Without thought, she opened the buttons on his front and the flesh sprang out, different from the statues she had seen in the books of ancient Greece.

She wished with all her might that she could touch it, feel it, bring it to her mouth and taste it. That thought shocked her, but then the whole day had been like that, the old clawing fear distant and harmless. She wanted to know him and move with him, this rhythm of sex a new knowledge and the unknown gripped her with an excitement that made her dizzy.

He brought her hand down across him, the warmth astonishing, the rigidity amazing. She felt it move as though it had a life of its own and he groaned. Power surged in her and she held on tighter as his breathing changed.

He was hers as much as she was his. She could bring him to the place of release with her ministrations just as easily as he had done to her with the kisses. An equal force, a shared potency.

On an instinct she licked her fingers and began to go faster.

She had him then as trapped as she had been and as immobile, his mouth opening, his eyes closing and his chest trembling with her touch.

Hers.

To love.

His rod drove through her fingers and spat out a liquid which filled her palm with heat.

'My God.' His words now. 'That has never happened before. Not like that.'

'It was wrong…?' She said this quietly. 'I hurt you?'

But he laughed and drew her in, kissing her cheeks and her chin and finally her mouth with a possession that was astonishing. Her breasts lay against his skin, his shirt opened now and warm, and she could feel his heart beat as easily as she could feel her own.

'No. You were wonderful, Mia. You made me forget…'

'I feel the same. With you it's as if it is only now that is important, this day, this afternoon, this night...'

'Will you stay with me until tomorrow?'

'Yes.'

'No one will look for us here. It is safe.'

The small clock in the corner sounded out the hour of two in the afternoon, but the day had darkened and outside Mia could hear the rain.

Augustus crossed to the bed and pulled back the covers, grabbing a woollen blanket from the wooden box at the foot and adding it as warmth before replacing the net. There was an opening in it that she had not seen before, a way of getting in, but allowing those there to stay hidden.

A perfect hideaway.

He found candles and placed them on the mantel near the bed, their light dancing in strange ways through the net. Enticing. Like something from another time.

The girl she had been even a week ago would have drawn back, but within her now was a bright-edged desire that she could not douse. She wanted Augustus Rushworth, she wanted all the things his kisses promised because he offered her a way out of the darkness and into the light.

All she needed to do was to trust him.

'I have a scar on my right leg. There was an accident and I broke it and it never healed properly. My stepmother once said that it was ugly and that were I ever to be married I should make certain I wore my petticoats at night.' She needed to tell him all her defects before they started on what might happen next. She did not want him surprised or put off by her leg that would never again be perfect.

'And you believed her?'

'My father said my mother had a birthmark on the top of her leg and he wished that she hadn't. It was one of the only things he ever told me of her. She was eighteen when she married him and nineteen when she died so she had hardly started life.'

She was talking too much, she knew that, words rolling around on her tongue and falling out. Biting down on more, she stopped, horrified by the fact that she had told him things that had festered for years inside her, things that should never have been said.

In answer, he began to take off his shirt, the damage she had seen on his right hand continuing up on to his arm and almost to the shoulder. No small injury either, but large, badly healed scars, criss-crossing and curling into each other like brambles in a thicket.

Seeing her shock, he smiled.

'People have their journeys, Euphemia, written in blood on to their skin. Some have small stories and others have broad ones, but I should not wish mine gone for the world because in a sense these are what made me who I am.'

She burst into tears, her emotions raw from the pain he must have once endured and then the truth hit her. She had been worrying about the wrong things because she had believed the wrong people—her father, her stepmother, a society that had never known her at all. Yet here before her in all his glory, unashamed and unhidden, was a man who had not been chained by his past, but had triumphed over it, a man who was trying to show her without words what it was to form a future from loss.

She went to him and laid her fingers upon the ravaged skin and his hands came around her, loosening the linen tapers from their casing at her waist. She felt the weight of her clothing drop to the floor, pooling around her feet, and she took in a breath, but did not look down.

The scar on her leg ran from the side of one knee down to the middle of her calf in an unbroken thin white line, a tidy and quiet marking compared to his own. She was the most beautiful woman he had ever seen in his lifetime and he lifted her into his arms, the warmth of her against his skin welcome as he took her to his bed.

She lay still, waiting while he removed the last of his own clothing and joined her, replacing the nets so that the space inside was only theirs.

In India he had always slept bare because of the fierce heat and so he was used to being naked, but he could see from her stiffness that she was not. He lay beside her on his side, one arm propping him up and a finger on his other hand trailing along the skin at her throat. Her breast was still reddened and he smiled, liking that he had marked her as his already, his touch falling to the spot as he gentled such hurt. He wanted all of her, every square inch, her curves beautifully made and her long hair beneath her in a silken curtain.

He leaned forward, his tongue taking over the job that his finger had begun, a trail of moisture, from throat to breast. He liked that her nipples stood proud, two hardened buds of need.

Then he ventured lower, to her stomach and her rounded hips, noticing the way she moved, the rise and fall of her body as she pressed back, the sound of her breathing, the beat of her heart.

Opening her legs, he claimed the moist centre of her, one finger finding the heat and then joined by a second. Her hand brushed through his hair as he kept penetrating, feeling how she began to know in his onslaught some old, bone-deep truth of what would come next.

She felt the power in him, but also the gentleness, here in their tent of net and candlelight, here where the rain beat on the roof and her heart beat in her breast with a violent need greater than anything she had ever felt before.

He was dark and large, but there on the edge of tenderness sat resolve. He was experienced and skilful, she could feel it in his ministrations, a lover who knew how to please a woman, a man who could break down all inhibition.

Would he hurt her? Would it be quick? She was overthinking, she knew that, her brain taking the joy of all he was doing and questioning it.

Then he moved and his mouth replaced his fingers and everything changed, a sound ripping from her that was low and guttural, unlike her own, piercing the silence in the room with the carnal, no longer vigilant or controlled.

His tongue found a place that made echoes inside of her, rifling through flesh with an ache of need, a hot quick stab of recognition and of certainty. The urgency held her there, still, waiting, everything around them consigned to the unimportant, her whole being centred on the way he moved within her, filling a need that held no words.

She felt a throb as the places inside her moulded around him, holding him there, as much of a prisoner to it as she was. He touched her then in a way that banished stillness and she moved for him, not knowing quite what was happening, but trusting him. His mouth was gone now and his fingers were back, the other hand above them lying on her stomach and pressing down. She could feel where they joined through the small space of skin, inside and out, the quickening rub of him inciting a fierce and joyous heat, building upwards, a faster rhythm, a harder push, no quietness in his movements now but the drive of need that would not be deprived.

She heard his breathing and her own, their skin slickened by sweat and it came, soft and distant at first and then with a rush, a wild overpowering need to push and flow. Like water as it was let go from a dam and spilled across the ramparts in a full and frenzied rush, emptying her, releasing her, allowing all that held her as a whole to fall into pieces, shattering across his touch.

She could not move, but lay there afterwards, wondering if what had just happened was a normal thing, wondering why any woman would ever leave the bed of a skilled lover for the ordinariness of the world. She felt ripe and strong and womanly.

She felt invincible.

When his hand slipped from her body she heard the wetness of it, a small sound with a wealth of meaning. She wished he would stay there inside her for all the hours of the night. She felt swollen and sensitive and wicked and the unappeased hunger in his eyes as he looked at her made her hope.

'There is more?'

She said these words in a whisper because she knew that there was.

'Much more.' These words were given in a way that failed to sound like his, hoarse, breathless and desperate. He turned then and sat up against the headboard, bringing her up so that she was splayed across him, her legs open, his sex poised beneath.

She felt cold air against the wetness of her hidden parts and her breath was taken away because of it, pressing closer, wanting things she had no words for. The heat grew, flushing her blood and making her insides melt, the pull of a union so strong she could not bear to wait.

'I want you.' Her words. Words she had once thought she might never say.

He simply placed his hands on her hips and pulled her down over him, the hardness surprising. He stilled her for a second as he entered her, waiting for her to be accustomed to him, and then he lifted his own body up so that there was no air between them, his full length inside as he strained against moving.

Holding her there, he kissed her, deep and true and hard, her mouth wide open to him.

They were joined everywhere, not two people, but one. It was like an extension of who he was, no place that each of them started or stopped. Such urgency held her, but her body began to move even as his did, gentle at first and then faster, the rush of passion, the fever of craving, the rise and strength of a feeling that was more potent than the last one. She stiffened and waited as the aches of lust came in, holding him to her, close and hot and thick.

Afterwards, he laid her down beside him and spooned around her, holding her cradled in his body, both of them breathing heavily. Euphemia was astonished. She had gone from a woman who was afraid of everything to one who understood now all that she had been missing.

It was like a rebirth into a sensory world that promised colour, whereas before it had only ever been grey.

'Thank you.'

She said this to him in awe and felt him smile.

'I think it is I who should be saying that to you, Euphemia.' She felt his breath against her back, alive and real and warm, and the dream lover of the past was only a shallow nothing, a ghost against the presence of a flesh-and-blood man. 'I have never felt so contented in a woman's bed before.'

Her heartbeat fluttered in her throat after such an unexpected compliment.

'I wish we could start life here again, in this cottage, Mia, bound together by the weather, far away from London and making love in the daylight with the shadows of light falling across us.'

Raising his hand, she saw the shadows of the movement on her skin. A sanctuary and a shelter, but for how long?

He spoke of a new slate, another beginning, yet there were blots there, for she had told him nothing of the actions of his brother.

She did not wish to either, not here, not now. No, she wanted to enjoy this gift of a day without regret. She had been foolish once, she knew she had, but most of it had been his brother's fault and for the first time since it happened blame shifted and she saw her part in it was lessened.

It was time to look forward, to see what she could make with the whole of the rest of her life, the years suddenly shimmering before her in a way they never had before. But what did he want of her? She could not quite tell.

Lovers?

The word rolled around inside her. To do as they wanted with each other's bodies. To lie here by the fire and away from the rain and find again the delicious release of the sensual. She twisted around and saw him looking at her with an intensity that had her breathing fast.

He wanted her as much as she wanted him. Taking his hand, she placed it on her breast, pleased when his finger found the nipple and he began to play.

It would happen again; she could feel his sex hardening and his breath deepening and the heat between them rising.

It was gentler this time, as he slipped into her wetness from behind, not the desperation of before, but a new temperance.

'I want to be in you for hours,' he whispered, both hands now on her breasts, cupping them. They were tethered by lust and need, but also by something else this time. Love…if she could have named it, but she didn't.

He was deep within her and she could feel his largeness pushing, encased in her flesh, an aching hunger expanding into every corner of her body.

She was his and he was hers, to taste and savour.

Relaxing, she fell into him, her breath a ragged groan and her fingers clenching the mattress beneath her, trying to find a balance as he finally brought her to the heavens, spent and satisfied, before the wings of sleep allowed slumber.

It was dark when she woke and the fire had long since gone out, bringing a chill to the room. The little moonlight there allowed her to get her bearings and she saw Augustus standing against the window looking out. He was naked, his body strong and fine in moonlight.

As if he could sense her consciousness, he turned and smiled at her.

'It's almost midnight. We've slept for hours. Are you hungry?'

She was ravenously hungry and nodded.

'Then I will find us food.'

'You're going out in this?' She could hear the silence and knew that it must have snowed.

'I'll raid the kitchens and be straight back.' He was pulling on his breeches and boots, his coat buttoned over his bare chest.

She tried to remember the twists and turns of the track that had led between the big house and the cottage.

'And it will be safe in this weather?'

'Very.'

He leaned down and kissed the top of her nose and then cradled her cheek with his hand. She saw he had taken the bracelet off and was surprised because she could not remember him wearing it yesterday in bed either.

Then the door opened and closed and he was gone, a draught of cold air instead filling the warmth of the room.

Euphemia sat up, wincing at the soreness between her legs, but smiling, too. She felt swollen and wet and her hand went down to feel her flesh.

The world was at bay here, all the problems far away, the worry and fears, and the thought that she might never be happy was gone, disappeared after her one amazing day and night in the bed of Augustus Rushworth.

She did not care that he had said nothing of love or of the future because for the first time in her whole life she only needed this perfect present. He and she in bed, making love and knowing each other and rising to the heavens every time they came together, the glory and the delight unmeasurable.

Lying back against the pillows, she placed her hand on her stomach, listening to her body. Happiness held a joy that created heat and every tiny bit of her felt warmed. She moved her hips and found again that feeling deep inside that was a part of Augustus, so easily summoned, as it spread from the place between her legs into her stomach and then up further, her breath stilling, her head tipping back.

She felt all woman and wicked, a knowledge now that spoke of a power which was unquenchable. A feminine power so unexpected she was stunned.

Did others feel this, too, or was it just her in this perfect place with a man who knew exactly how to tend to her?

Augustus stood outside in the gardens in the cold and leaned back against a wall that was out of the wind.

He could not believe what had just happened to him, a man who had been sure that the world held no more surprises and that his life was from now on to be defined by duty, obligation and responsibility.

Euphemia Denniston had astonished him with her generosity and her sensuality. She had been a virgin and yet she had not held back, nor had she insisted on commitment or contract.

She had given her body without strings attached, joyfully and wholly. She had matched him in passion, step by step, too, which was something that had never happened before.

'Hell.' He closed his eyes and raised his face to the sky, feeling the small soft drifts of snow land upon his skin. He had taken her as he might a mistress and she did not deserve such a thing. He had used her as a whore and she had gone along with it, in innocence and inexperience.

He had behaved exactly like his brother.

That thought had him pushing away from his shelter. His brother was a man who he'd sworn he would never emulate, a man who cared not a jot for others, but only for his own self-satisfaction.

The anger left him abruptly, but shame took its place. How could he fix this? How could he make it right?

By courting her properly, by taking her back to London and gaining permission from her stepmother to escort her to the great events of the forthcoming Season. By making sure that her reputation was not ripped to shreds by everyone who had the desire to comment, by being honourable and moral and decent as he had not been thus far, rushing her into a bed in the cottage on the estate with all the lust in the world.

He looked up at the sky, the moon scudding behind clouds, the ground thick with new snow, his footprints marking where he had tracked.

In the kitchen he gathered fresh rolls and ham and cheese, apples, a knife, a plate and a large slice of the

pound cake that was one of the cook's signature reci-
pes. He placed them all in a basket he found on one
side of the bench.

When he returned to the cottage she was up, a blanket wrapped around her shoulders and covering her
whole body, her hair falling in wisps around her face
and then far down her back in a long wheaten curtain.

Like an angel.

More guilt surfaced, but he smiled because he saw
her worry.

'I hoped you had not got lost out there in the snow,
August.'

'I am here now.'

He laid the food on the table, but she did not cross
over to see what was there. Rather she stood and
watched him as he removed his coat, the scars on his
arms standing out in the light of the candles which she
had burning.

'You must have been very sick?'

'I was.' He did not wish to talk of this, not now, not
with the thoughts of his brother so close. It would be like
a summoning of old ghosts and he brushed her words
away, pleased to banish the past into the darkness.

Her eyes left him and he saw the way her fingers
clenched the wool. Unsure but brave.

She continued speaking. 'What happened here in
this room is between us. If you are worried I should
insist on promises...'

'I am not.'

And that was the whole trouble. She had been surviving all her life on small miserable crumbs and here he was throwing her some more.

'You are beautiful, Euphemia, and every moment I lay with you was more wonderful than the last. But I should not have expected what I did and I am sorry for—'

She crossed the room and placed one finger on his lips to stop the words. Then she dropped her blanket.

'Take me again here on the floor. That is what I want, August. Only that.'

Food was forgotten, his mouth drying in the face of such an invitation. He reached out and brought her down, mounting her quickly and without preamble, watching her smile.

This time he took her with no thought of his brother or of his duty or even of his ruminations in the snow ten minutes before.

He took her like a man who knew he had found his destiny and who understood that this woman would always be his, no matter what, his to care for and love and cherish. He took her because he knew the turn of destiny and the place of karma and of the samsara and of an escape from the impermanence he had always lived in.

He hoped he might impregnate her so that she would be tied to him, this woman of kindness and honesty and courage. He wanted her to be happy, to have a place and a family. He wanted to be in her life for ever, to have a brood of children, to grow old together laughing through the years, history woven between them into eternity.

He pushed in so hard he felt the neck of her womb against his manhood and his seed spilled and spilled and spilled inside her.

She lay there, the last waves of release pounding through her, the ache of his urgency branding her flesh in a way that made her take in breath and wish it could begin all over again.

But she was spent, like him, lost at the edge of exhaustion and awe.

This was something she could never have dreamed of from the quiet cold of her upstairs bedroom, where she'd lain awake and alone every night, hoping for something else, something better.

This.

She did not wish to move. She wanted to stay here with him on top of her, heavy, sheltering her, covering her, making her whole again, quickening her blood.

Perfect.

The word came like a mantra.

Karma. The belief he had told her of about rebirth and the sewing of seeds for future happiness. The deep ache in her womb echoed the hope of it.

When he stood and lifted her up again to the soft mattress, she smiled.

In the morning she felt his distance and his desire to be gone. He had had the carriage brought round as soon as they were dressed, not stopping for breakfast or to enter the estate.

The cream façade of Stanthorpe Hall in the snow looked like a fairy-tale castle, a place that held the secrets of the Rushworths within it, yet breathed in a beauty that was calming. She wished with all her heart that they might have stayed.

As they wound back up the long drive she turned to look again, the trees framing the house now, bare-stick and brown.

Oaks, she decided by their shape, and ancient ones at that.

If August noticed her looking, he did not say so and she wondered if he was angry at her. What would happen when they got back to London? Was the pact they had concocted still a part of their relationship?

It was her birthday today, too, but he seemed to have forgotten. She kept that fact to herself, her thirty-first year heralded in silence, a marking of the passing of time only, another way to see a future that might not hold Augustus Rushworth in it.

He had said she was beautiful and that every moment he had lain with her had been more wonderful than the last. But he had also said that he should not have expected what had happened and that he was sorry for it.

Was that a careful way to tell her that he regretted what had happened? His sorrow angered her because he'd had every chance to turn things in another direction and he had participated in their couplings with as much vigour as she had.

She was disappointed in his lack of honesty, as well,

but too tired to plead otherwise. For the first time ever in his company, she just wanted to be out of it.

They did not leave the carriage at the inn. Rather, the servant scurried to find them food and they ate it as they went, Augustus's glance taking in all those who arrived at the roadside tavern around them and pulling the heavy curtains closed if they came too near.

Was he ashamed of her? Did he not wish to be seen in her company now that he had discovered everything that had until last night been hidden? Her nipples were sensitive after his ministrations and when she moved and one breast brushed up against the scratchy wool of her gown she grimaced.

'You are hurt?' He sounded furious.

She shook her head and looked away and he did not pursue the conversation, the miles eaten up in silence and the sleet outside making it hard to speak.

An hour later they were back in the busier streets of London, the countryside left well behind. She wondered if he would take her to his place, but the destination became clear when the driver turned towards Bolton Street.

He would see her home and then he would go straight to Doctors' Commons and procure a special licence in order that he might marry her as soon as he could. There was nothing else for it to save her name and to salvage all the mistakes he had made.

She was quiet this morning and had barely looked at him, her fingers running over the wool in her cloak this way and that in a nervous gesture.

He had hurt her, he could tell from the way she moved and from the way she had blushed a bright red when he had asked her about it.

Worst thing of all, if she had allowed him even the tiniest of encouragement he would have tugged her on to his knees, lifted her skirts and taken her, there in the carriage with the streets of London just outside, at a time when the servants could have opened the door at any moment and found them, coupled and replete. Even the thought of it made him feel sick, but his manhood rose regardless and he could do nothing to stop it.

'I will take you home now, Euphemia, but this evening I shall be back and we will need to talk.'

'Talk?' The word was said softly, almost whispered.

'There is much I have to say and explain, but it would be better when I have had time to do what I must and then things will become clearer.'

'To you?'

'To us both.'

A shout from outside brought his face to the window and his man veered the carriage to the side of the road, the modest Denniston dwelling behind it.

The door opened and he helped her out, careful to keep his hands away from her lest those who were walking by observe him. Then she was on the footpath and he could see the boy at the front door. Augustus bowed to her in a way that was mannered and appropriate and she was gone, turned to the steps, her bright blue eyes lost to him, the wind lifting her plaited hair.

Once inside Euphemia crossed the front lobby into the salon and sat in the small blue chair, her hat in her hand and her cloak still on.

She was back home and Augustus was lost to her, gone on into his life in the manner she had always known that he would, and away from her.

Yet she had returned a different woman, a woman who had known what it was to love and be loved, sensually and completely. Her insides throbbed at just the thought and her nipples hardened. To anyone else she would be seen as ruined should they have had any inkling as to how she had spent her last night, but to her she was renewed, no longer the old and drab Miss Euphemia Denniston, but a woman who had been brought back to life by the sensual.

Holding her hands up, she saw them shake and then her fingers felt for the ring he had given her beneath her clothing. A ruby, and powerful.

She would return the jewellery and the clothes, of course, the earrings still tucked in with her pearls, another present she must make certain to get back to him.

She knew what he would say to her this evening, for how could she not?

He would say he was thankful for her gift and for the help she had given him. He would say that she was beautiful and the hours they had spent in the cottage on his grandmother's estate would always be precious.

But he would also tell her of his duties to marry well and produce an heir, something which at her age might not be possible. He would wish her the best and probably try to give her money, but she would refuse this, allowing him to leave on terms of friendship and amity.

It would be a cordial parting that would permit survival. For her. She knew that if she went to pieces at his leaving she might never regain her wholeness and she was determined to keep the strength that he had given her intact.

'August.' She whispered his name and then stood, moving towards the stairs. Once inside her room, she locked the door and found the pitcher of water and a cloth.

She would wash herself and put on different clothing. When she glanced at the mirror after undressing, she was amazed to see the ways he had marked her, with his kisses at her throat, with the redness of her nipples, and with the slight graze down one thigh where the floor had been hard as he had thrust again and again to take her to oblivion.

One hand went to the place of wetness between her legs and she drew it up, assessing the liquid which was musky and salty.

She took a cloth and soap and began to wash him away.

Augustus arrived back home just as Tobias Balcombe did and he appeared a bit rattled.

'I'm pleased to finally find you here, August, as I

have attempted to speak with you a number of times over the last day, but you haven't been home.'

'What were you wanting me for?' He was not really in the mood for distraction as he needed to find the ring his grandmother had given him as a wedding band for Euphemia and he was also desperate to get to Doctors' Commons.

'I ran into Lord Bambury last night. He knows I am a friend of yours and he proceeded to make noises about the promised union between your families. It seems his daughter is a girl of four-and-twenty and is still unmarried and he is beginning to be more than concerned. The fact that you have returned to England and paraded Miss Denniston in society has not pleased him either and I would not be surprised if he demands to see you before very long in order to settle the matter.'

'God.' He knew the name and he knew the promise, but after ten years abroad and a previous marriage he had also presumed it would be null and void.

Still, he was enough of a diplomat to know that small misunderstandings such as this had the propensity to develop into painful rifts and long-held grudges and he needed to nip such an idea in the bud before it blossomed into something he had no control over. His recent night with Euphemia made the whole issue more urgent still.

'Where does Lord Bambury reside now?'

'More normally in London, but he left for his brother's home in Holloway just this afternoon.'

'Damn.'

'You seem more flustered than I have ever seen you? What the hell is wrong?'

'I am not interested in the daughter of Lord Bambury, but there is another woman whom I have wronged and such dishonour needs to be rectified.'

'I am presuming the lady you are speaking of is Miss Euphemia Denniston?'

'How could you know that?'

'How could anyone not? You looked at her the other evening as if she were a tasty morsel that you couldn't wait to try.'

Augustus sat down on the seat in his office where they had now retired. 'She was much more than that to me. I spent last night with her and she was a virgin.'

'I take it then that she no longer is one?'

'You take it correctly.'

'So you have the difficulty of an old, unwanted promise and the chance of a new, wonderful one? If you rode up to Holloway, you could be there in under an hour, speak to Bambury and set him right and then return by the evening to rectify the problem you have with Miss Denniston. My horse is saddled outside and more than ready for a good ride, for I meant to take him down to Rotten Row after seeing you. Bambury's brother's residence is the third substantial country house on the left-hand side after the crossroads in the town.'

'You know the Bamburys that well?'

'The twenty-four-year-old hopeful is my cousin three times removed and, although I like her, I think you would make a lucky escape should you enlighten her father on your plan to wed another. He is a reasonable man. More so than his daughter, at least.'

'Thank you, Tobias.'

'I want you to be as happy as I am, August, and with the wife you were meant to have.'

Grabbing his hat, gloves and cloak, Augustus strode outside and was pleased to see Tobias's mount was every bit as magnificent as he had made him out to be.

Thirty-five minutes there, one hour at the most with Bambury and thirty-five minutes home. Yes, he looked at the timepiece at his waist. He could get to see Euphemia before seven o'clock and even if he didn't have the damn licence he was going to ask her to marry him anyway and he would not be taking no for an answer.

The noise downstairs began to get louder. There was a shouting and screaming and the banging of doors and her name being called in a shrill and accusatory manner.

'Euphemia? Euphemia? Where are you?'

She had fallen asleep after dressing and was instantly off her bed.

Lucille and Susan were back? The world blackened for a second as a result of her quick rise and she held on to the side table.

'Euphemia!' Another shout and then they were at her door, their mouths agog when they saw the golden gown in its hanging on the hook at the front of the wardrobe and the accompanying slippers and cloak.

'It is true, then.' Lucille's voice held a censure that

was more worrying than the screams. 'All the gossip we have heard of you is true.'

She could not answer.

'You stole Mr Rushworth from me,' Susan shouted now, a great temper in her words. 'You sent us to Bath because you wanted him for yourself. I can't believe you would do that.'

The quick slap on her face from Lucille was unexpected and hard. Euphemia reeled back to stand out of the way as her stepmother began where Susan had left off.

'You did not come home last night, either, but left yesterday morning in the company of Augustus Rushworth. Bobby has just informed us of the whole. He also said you had been giddy with the excitement of a ball you attended in Rushworth's company.'

'It was not like that…' Mia had finally found her voice, but was interrupted.

'You did not stay with him overnight?'

Mia remained still.

Lucille had gained traction now and she crossed the room and tore the golden gown from its sheath of calico. 'This is yours? Mr Rushworth brought you this? Well, if your reputation was in tatters before it shall now be more so. The foolish spinster daughter of a man who could never keep his hands to himself and a daughter who appears to be just as permissive. A family trait. You shall be laughed out of London, Euphemia Denniston, and you should be. Now get out. Gather your things and get out and never darken our doorway again with your lying and guile and deceit. To think you sent us off with full knowledge of what you had planned with him makes me sick.'

Susan looked shocked by her mother's words, but she said nothing.

The servants were in the hallway watching, the two who had been left behind and the two who had been taken to Bath. Euphemia knew that her story would be all over London come the morning and she could do nothing about it.

She gathered up the thick wool cloak and dug out the pearl earrings August had given her and her mother's necklace and shoved them into her pocket.

The fury of her stepmother washed over her and she was careful to stay out of striking range of Lucille as she left. She did not even say goodbye.

Once outside, she put on her hat and cloak and made for the town house of August Rushworth in St James's.

He had not returned to see her, though it was not full evening yet, but she needed to tell him what had happened—not because she expected anything from him, but because after their night together she felt she owed him some explanation.

The shock of the past few moments had left her feeling ill, a nausea arising in her stomach as she considered her options. With night coming on, the world looked scary and huge, the shadows gathering all around and the rain beginning again.

Where would she sleep? Where could she go? She had her mother's pearls to take to a pawnshop if she had to, but after that? She had never been out on her own like this before, out in a world that might not be kind to a woman who had not adhered to the rules of society. She had broken every code and yet she was still not sorry. No, she strode across the street at a faster pace and looked neither left nor right. She would never be sorry for her one perfect night with Augustus Rushworth and that was just how it was. Feeling tears pool in her eyes, she wiped them away in irritation and hurried on.

Augustus was not at home and the servant at the door was haughty and dismissive.

'The master is not expected back till late, and in fact...' his eyes scanned the gathering night behind her '...the likelihood is he may not even return till the morrow.'

She saw in his expression disapproval and condemnation and knew it was not done for an unmarried woman, no matter how old, to simply turn up alone and uninvited on the doorstep of a gentleman.

'I shall, however, tell him that you have called, Miss Denniston.'

She nodded. 'Thank you. Could you please give him these?'

She took the ancient earrings in their box from her pocket and handed them over. For a second she saw something akin to puzzlement in his face, a bafflement that softened irritation.

'I shall.'

'Thank you.'

The door shut as she turned and she was left looking out on to a city at night that was dangerous and unknown. The thought crossed her mind then that if she were to be robbed, at least Augustus would have his priceless family heirlooms back. One hand clutched her mother's pearls with fervour as she stepped out on to the street.

Chapter Eleven

Tobias's horse had thrown a shoe and Augustus's heart sank at the implications of such a thing for there was no chance now of visiting Euphemia this evening.

He should have sent word to her before he left, but he had not, wanting the surprise of it all when he went down on his knee and asked her to marry him. She must be expecting such a proposal, was his next thought, even if she had never said a word, for what well brought-up woman would imagine a gentleman would not understand his responsibilities and ask for her hand in marriage after taking her virginity.

He had spent as little time with Bambury as was acceptable, disavowing his father's conditions of an alliance with as much politeness as he could muster, and thankfully the man had understood perfectly. The offer now formally withdrawn, he had then got back on the horse again in the thickening snow and made for London, only to have the steed throw a shoe and now he was sitting in a tavern having a drink and waiting for the smithy to finish with the horse.

If Tobias knew of this old offer of an alliance between him and the twenty-four-year-old Miss Bambury, then he wondered who else also knew of it. He hoped like hell that Euphemia did not hear about it and start to imagine things that had never been true.

His thoughts returned to Euphemia and he smiled. He had never met a woman as responsive as she was in the bedroom and one who actually seemed to like the act of sex. How on earth had she managed with her temperament to get to the ripe old age of thirty and still be a virgin?

Another thought came after that one, a sort of lost and jumbled association. Thirty-one. Her birthday. It was today and he had forgotten entirely with every other thing that was happening.

He had to get back to London. He had to see her. He had to move heaven and earth to find a conveyance or a horse that would get him south in the very quickest of times and he would knock on the door of her Bolton Street house no matter what the hour might be.

He was no longer worried about the licence or about the ring. He would offer himself to her and then go with her to his grandmother's estate until he could find a priest to tie the knot and make sure she was his for ever.

A sound behind him had him turning and there, wending his way through a group of locals, was Tony Ferris.

'August?' There was a tone in his voice which suggested he was seeing a mirage. 'I saw Tobias's horse in the smithy's yard and the man said a Mr Rushworth was inside and as I had heard you were home I was hoping it might be you.'

Reaching him, he slapped his friend hard on the back and whooped in delight. 'I can't believe you are here. In England. When on earth did you get back?'

'The first day of February. I came in during the Frost Fair. Are you going down to London?'

'I am on the way back now. Can I give you a ride? I can leave one of my men to bring the horse back if it suits you and then you won't have to wait.'

Ten minutes later, ensconced in a fast-moving carriage, August was very much relieved.

'What are you doing in Camden Town, anyway?' Tony appeared perplexed.

'It's complicated.'

A shout of laughter ensued. 'When the hell wasn't it with you, August? It's not your grandfather, is it? Did he recall you under oath of cutting you off if you didn't reappear?'

'No, though in some sense he is to blame. My father was keen to pursue a union with Lord Bambury's daughter and years ago set up a promise between our family and theirs. When Tobias told me of Bambury's hopes of it I travelled up to see him in Holloway to let him know I would not be bound by my father's promise.'

'How did Lord Bambury take it?'

'Surprisingly well, actually. I think he appreciated my coming.'

'A Miss Euphemia Denniston has taken your eye, I also hear? My cousin James was at the Barretts' ball and I have just seen him at Oxford. He regaled me with an account of this fair lady as the belle of the occasion and you looked most taken with her.'

'Now that is accurate.'

'The thing is that while he was talking about Miss Denniston I had the impression that my aunt may have known her mother well. She certainly asked James many questions about the daughter.'

'Her mother died when she was born and she lost touch with her other relatives.'

'Well, according to my aunt the family tried to find them and they looked hard.'

'Really? What was the relative's name?'

'Aunt Caroline didn't mention it, but you could follow it up with her if you want. She lives near Liverpool and was due to leave for Oxford an hour or so after I did, but she said she'd sent word to the family this morning just in case they did not know. She asked me for your address so that the connection might be clearer for them to follow.'

'And where do these people live?'

'I think Aunt Caroline said it was close to London.'

'Well, I certainly hope they do turn up, for Euphemia would be delighted to know them. I shall let her know of your aunt's knowledge of her mother's family as soon as I see her.'

'You sound happy, August. Happier than I remember you.'

'That's because I am.'

Once home and through the front door, his butler thrust the pearl earrings he had given Euphemia into his hands, his face lined with worry.

'I think, sir, that there has been a grave mistake made. Miss Denniston knocked at the door in the late afternoon and asked if you were home. When I told her you had gone out of town for the day she placed these earrings into my hands and bade me to make sure you received them. The thing is, Mr Rushworth, that I did not know that she was the woman you had taken to Stanthorpe House. It was the lad in the kitchen who set me right, sir, as he had been sent to Miss Denniston's house on Bolton Street with some clothes the day before the Barretts' ball. He also said he had seen her leaving the house after she brought the earrings back, sir, and saw her getting into a carriage that had pulled up in the road in front of her. I sent him to the same house in Bolton Street to enquire after her welfare, but the owner there, a Mrs Lucille Denniston, said she had run off after an argument and that she was missing.'

'Missing?'

'Miss Denniston left of her own accord, according to the younger daughter, after they returned unexpectedly from Bath. Mrs Denniston said Miss Euphemia Denniston told them that she was ashamed at what she had done and that her reputation was now in tatters.

Apparently they themselves had visitors soon after she had left and they were not…discreet.'

It was getting worse. Had she truly told them she was ashamed at what had happened between them? He could not believe that she would, but now Euphemia was lost in London somewhere. On top of that, by to-morrow, the whole *ton* would know of her downfall, or at least know of her stepmother's version of the facts.

And it was all his fault.

Had she been kidnapped, or could it have been some-one she knew who had seen her and helped her?

'Send a messenger to the homes of the Balcombes, the Baker-Hills and the Forsythes, asking them if they have any knowledge of where Miss Denniston is. And, Higgins, did she seem upset when she arrived here?'

'No, she came to ask if you were at home and I said you were not and I had no idea when you would be back. She did not ask if she could wait, sir, though in retro-spect I perhaps should have offered it.'

Dismissing the man, Augustus went into his library, but he could not settle. Where the hell had she gone? She had no family, no friends and little money. Fury and worry vied equally with each other as he poured himself a drink and looked out of the window. It was dark outside now, there was no moon to speak of and damn cold. There could not have been a worse night for Euphemia to be lost in London than this one. He breathed in deeply and tried to think.

Bram and Rupert turned up half an hour later and Tobias and Tony another twenty minutes after that. No one had seen Euphemia, but the rumours of what had happened between them had become known everywhere. He cursed the loose-tongued stepmother to hell and refused the food brought in by one of the footmen.

It was a disaster and he sent his carriage and driver around the streets of London to look for her. Tony left for Oxford almost as soon as he had arrived to quiz his aunt on Euphemia's mother's family and his other friends went to check the boarding houses nearby. He himself wanted to stay at home in case she came back.

The clock struck nine and then ten, hollow, empty sounds calling out the passage of time. He could not bear to speak of what might have happened, thoughts of his own near mugging the night he had arrived in London coming back in force.

By mid-morning the next day he had concocted a plan. He shaved, washed and dressed carefully and then he called for his carriage. It would be better to address the carnage of Euphemia's damaged reputation than to sit here and let it be picked to pieces by all the unkind gossipmongers of the *ton*. It was his fault, all of this, after all. But first he would visit Tobias.

White's was busy when they arrived and he was glad of it. More ears to listen, more people to scurry home to more households with the salubrious gossip he was about to impart.

Gluing an expression on his face that held an equal measure of surprise and anger, he strode into the room and found Roddy Thistlewaite at the bar. Exactly the right person. A tattletale of the umpteenth degree.

In India he had been applauded for his diplomacy and yet here with Euphemia he seemed to have forgotten his skills completely. Well, that was all about to change.

'Rushworth.' Roddy Thistlewaite's voice was smug. 'There are rumours going around about your ladybird?'

'My ladybird?' August placed a question mark at the end and waited.

'Miss Euphemia Denniston. It seems from all accounts she has crossed the boundaries of propriety and erred on the side of the carnal.'

August stayed still, garnering the attention of the room before continuing. 'And me? What is it they say of my behaviour?'

'I don't understand?'

The club quietened now and August could feel the listening ears all about him.

'I want to make certain that you know that I was part of the equation, too.'

'What are you getting at?'

'I am getting at the fact that Miss Denniston was well chaperoned and treated most courteously. We travelled up to the Stanthorpe estate in a group and I made certain that she was treated with the respect she deserved.'

'My wife Anna was there, Thistlewaite, and everyone knows she is a stickler for doing the right thing.'

Tobias said this just as they had planned that he would and if by any chance some soul did disprove the story, he would have found Euphemia by then and married her. It was a way forward until he could ask her.

The voices of those around them began to hum in the background and Augustus could feel the lines of gossip reaching out. His interest in Euphemia Denniston would be common knowledge across London come the morning and that was just the way he wanted it.

But Thistlewaite was not quite finished. 'I have heard from close sources that Miss Denniston has left London and disappeared into the ether?'

'Unfortunately that is true, but she has told me she needs some time to consider her options and I have respected that.'

'A woman who has no connections, money or family, needs time to think about such a thing? I don't know how you think anyone will swallow that tale, Rushworth…'

August hit him then, square across the jaw, and he fell quite gracefully for such a big man, lying still on the floor in front of his feet as the room erupted into motion, the words he had said nowhere near as convincing as his action.

'Thistlewaite never was a man who understood the ways of the heart.'

Tobias's words were measured and calm and people around them nodded in agreement.

The danger was past, August thought, but still he needed to make certain of it.

'If anyone else has something to say, I'd like to hear it now.'

'Congratulations on finding a woman who is worth all the fuss, Rushworth. The next drink is on me.'

Lance Sedgwick gave him these words, the man's face full of a genuine gladness and August tipped his head in thanks as Tobias grabbed two glasses, lifting his own in amusement.

'To love,' he said, 'and may yours run as smoothly as mine did.'

August laughed at that, the tension in him abating as he remembered the run-around Anna had given his friend.

Tobias might know the truth, but no one else would, and as Thistlewaite removed himself from the place with a decided fury he plastered a smile on his face.

He had protected Euphemia. Now all he had to do was to find her as quickly as he could and bring her home to marry her.

Euphemia sat in the beautiful formal gardens of Benningbrook Hall and watched over the extensive parklands beyond, the pale meadows undulating against the darker trees that crouched in the groins of the hills.

Her mother must have sat here, writing or reading or simply watching all those years ago, when she was young and the world was at her feet.

Elizabeth had not been anything like Euphemia had imagined. Here, she came fully alive, in portraits and in old jottings and in the stories her great-aunts and uncle told her. Here, her mother had ridden bareback across the land, climbed the largest trees to one side of the house and made up complex theatrical productions complete with costumes for a family who'd adored her.

Her Great-Aunt Adeline came from the house now, a servant behind her carrying two cups of tea on a tray together with fresh scones and jam from the kitchen, a daily ritual that was a calming one. Adeline was her mother's aunt and she made a point of telling Mia that they had been close right up until the day Elizabeth had left.

'Her own mother had passed away, you see, quite early, so I was in effect a replacement and it gave me so much joy to be so. You look like her, you know, my darling,' she said after a moment from her seat opposite once the servant had left. 'You have the same vibrant beauty as Elizabeth did, the sort that stops people in their tracks and makes them look twice. It was why I came to St James's Square in the first place the other day, because my great friend, Edith Monroe, told me that Mr Rushworth had escorted a Miss Denniston to the Barretts' ball who looked uncannily like Elizabeth did when she was young and she thought it was well worth a visit to Rushworth to be able to discount such a coincidence. In fact, I had another note this very morning from an old friend from Liverpool and she was most insistent I look into the matter as well.'

A warm but wizened hand came across her own, holding on as Mia looked over, and she was transported back to that dreadful evening two nights before when she had been thrown out on the street, first by her stepmother and then by the haughty Rushworth butler.

The carriage that had been passing her in St James's Square as she had left Augustus's home had slowed and a woman had alighted, an older woman with white hair and a beautiful face who was smiling at Mia as if she had discovered a pot of gold at the end of a rainbow.

A servant had stood beside her in livery, a man almost as ancient as the woman was and he'd made certain she did not fall as she took the last step down.

'Are you by any chance Miss Euphemia Denniston?' the old woman had asked as Mia stopped to watch what was happening and she had nodded.

'Then I need to talk with you most urgently, for I believe you are my niece's long-lost daughter. Elizabeth Caughey. Do you recognise that name?'

'Who are you?'

Euphemia was bewildered, tumbled from one surprise to the next, tossed by the unpredictable like a small feather in a very strong wind.

'I am Lady Adeline Stanton, from Benningbrook Park. Perhaps your mother has had a hand in facilitating this meeting from her place above in Heaven, for she was always a girl with a good sense of humour and a great grasp of the absurd.'

The words made Euphemia breathe in deeply.

'Libby, we called her that, was inclined to spur-of-the-moment decisions, you see. We could never quite bridle her exuberance and when she met Mr Lionel Denniston and married him after only a few weeks it was understood the relationship would likely be fraught with problems. This is no slight to your father, my dear, no slight at all, it is just that a girl who meets and marries a man in the space of only a matter of days has the odds of happiness running against her, would you not say?'

Mia added up the days in her head since she had met and slept with Augustus Rushworth and declined to answer. Like mother, like daughter. The phrase whirred in her head, round and round like a ditty.

'We heard Libby had died less than a year after she left here because your father wrote to tell us of it and of the birth of their baby daughter. But then Lionel Denniston disappeared with you in tow and there was never another letter. The world simply swallowed you both up and every effort to locate you came to nothing. Until now, and here you are, like a prayer that has finally been answered.'

As if she had only just realised the weather was worsening, she gestured to the waiting carriage.

'Would you join me inside, my dear, so that we may keep talking without freezing, for I am afraid at my age I feel the cold?'

A moment later Mia was in the carriage, bundled into a large pile of blankets and plied with a tumbler of drink that was the strongest thing she had ever tasted.

'To chase away the cold, my dear, and the chance of sickening with it. A Benningbrook tradition from way back and there are so many more of them. Oh, I can't wait until Terence, my brother, and my cousin Jennifer see you. They will not believe who I have brought home and they shall be as glad as I am and as enchanted.

Neither of them married, you see, so our world is a small one.'

All these words tumbled into Mia's head: family, a place, a world that she had always dreamed of and never known.

'Our family hails from Sevenoaks in Kent. Benning-brook Park is an old estate near the Greensand Hills and your Great-Uncle Terence is the Earl of Aldridge. Do any of these names mean anything to you?'

'No, I am sorry.'

'Don't be sorry, my dear. It is we who must apologise for not finding you sooner and bringing you home where you belong. We employed a man years ago when your mother first left so that we might see how she fared, but he was able to deduce very little. I think, in retrospect, that we had coddled Libby too much after her mother and father died, so freedom was a heady elixir and a new marriage meant she had other things to think about. I only hope she was happy.'

Mia had been here at Benningbrook Park for two days now, in the heart of a family—her family—that was attentive and kind. She had hardly surfaced for the first day because everything had caught up with her and she was exhausted. But today, here, with her great-aunt's hand cradling her own, she could not believe how fortunate she had been.

'I do have a question that I need to ask you, Euphemia, much as I wish I did not.'

'A question?' She could tell by her tone that her aunt was worried about something.

'There are rumours that are circulating about you in London that have reached us here this morning by way of a neighbour. They are damning rumours, unfortunately, and so it is with trepidation that I ask now how well you know Mr Rushworth?'

Euphemia felt a slice of terror run through her because with her great-aunt she would have to be honest and she did not quite know what the result might be.

'I spent a day and a night with him...in his bed.'

The words fell into silence and she could not even look up.

Until now she had not had the slightest of regrets about what had happened between them. All she could think of was the wonder of it, the beauty of their hours away from everyone and the way her body had responded to his.

But here with her old aunt looking so frail, a new shame surfaced, a knowledge that what they had done was so far from acceptable in the eyes of society governed by manners and propriety that she might never again be able to fit in.

As if seeing her terror, her aunt leant in closer.

'I am not here to judge you, Euphemia, not after such a long time of having you lost to us. My prime purpose in life now is to keep you safe.'

'I am not sure that is possible...'

Her words were tossed away summarily. 'Of course it is. We are far from the city and you need never go back to London again no matter what they say of you. This world here is ours to control and we love you. Nothing will alter that. I speak for the entire family. You are Elizabeth's daughter and you have a home here for however long you want it. For ever, I hope. Now, how would you like us to handle Rushworth?'

'Handle him?'

'He broke the rules, my dear. He did not treat you as he should have and for a man of that standing there must be consequences. Do you want us to insist he marry you? We could do that with barely the blink of an eye.'

'No.' The word was torn from her without thought.

'Because he hurt you? Because you do not like him?'

Tears she had not cried before streamed down her cheeks at the question. 'It is, in fact, the very opposite, Aunt Adeline, but...'

'But what?'

'I am no longer a young woman and before I came here the options available to me were sorely limited. He did not drag me to his bed.'

Her great-aunt nodded and straightened up. 'Very well. Do you love him? I think that must be my next question.'

'More than life itself and he is a good man, I know it.'

'Did you tell him that? Tell him of your feelings for him?'

'No, because although he said that I was beautiful he also said that he should not have expected what happened between us and that he was sorry for it.'

'The bedding?'

She nodded and felt the blush rise in her cheeks. 'I

have disappointed you and that is the last thing I want to do.'

'Never apologise for love, my dear, and if Rushworth does not return your feelings then it is his loss and he is the one you should feel sorry for. One day he shall weep rivers of tears for such a mistake, I know it.'

Her words were so far from how she saw Augustus that Mia had to stifle a smile. It was good to have someone like Aunt Adeline so firmly on her side and she swallowed, trying to find her composure.

She was safe here and happy and it was so long since she had been able to say that. No, that was a lie, too, for in August's arms she had known joy beyond belief.

'I knew Mr Rushworth's grandfather once and he was a difficult man. The father and the grandson had their critics, too, but I did not hear the same said of the younger Rushworth boy. Is he the one who disappeared off to India?'

'Yes.'

'And returned just recently with a fortune?'

'He did.'

'Then you have good taste, but if you do not wish to pursue him and would like another, we shall find you a suitor from around these parts who will make a fine husband.'

'No. I will never marry.'

'Well, that is your right, too, my dear, and the years of women having to be wives by necessity are fading with the new century and thank goodness for that.'

Euphemia was astonished by her aunt's liberal views.

'Were you ever wed, Aunt Adeline?'

'Once, a long time ago, but my husband died and my heart died with him, so I never looked at another man again.'

'Then I shall be just like you.'

Her aunt looked thoughtful. 'Where there is life there is always hope, Euphemia, remember that. But for now let us enjoy our tea and scones.'

Every meal thus far had been wonderful here at Benningbrook and with no expense spared. When she looked back at her life in London she could only think of how meagrely they had eaten at the house on Bolton Street.

'Do the others know of these rumours?' She could barely imagine what her ancient Great-Uncle Terence might think and Cousin Jennifer, while some years younger than Adeline, must be nearing eighty herself.

'They do and they think as I do. You have a home here and the Park, though reasonably close to London, is a place where the world leaves us alone. Like a fortress that cannot be breached unless we wish it to be. If you do not mind, I shall relate our conversation here to Terence and Jennifer. I have always found good, honest communication to be the answer to most problems, my dear.'

Was Adeline offering another piece of advice in her veiled words? Perhaps she should send August a letter explaining her side of things, telling him where she was now for, after all, she had promised him honesty.

But not just yet. She needed another day to simply

think and be. A day, too, to get to know all she could about her mother, and later this morning Aunt Adeline was going to take her to the attic and show her all the things that had been boxed up when her mother had died.

She hoped there might be a journal or something in which she could find some guidance for her own situation. She had seen the paintings of Elizabeth and the sketches and every time she did so she was astonished at how many physical similarities there were between them.

'How did my father meet my mother?'

'Lionel Denniston came because Terence sent for him. Your father was an academic and well known in the circles of London's bookish set. Terence felt that Benningbrook Park needed its library catalogued and Mr Denniston arrived in the summer of 1782 when Elizabeth had just turned eighteen. I think she fell in love with him the day he arrived, though he was not a demonstrative man so I could never tell exactly what he thought of her.'

'And they left soon after?'

'Eloped two weeks later. Ran for the Scottish border and married the moment they got there. We knew right then and there that we had lost her.'

Mia had never heard of this. Not once had her father told her one word of their adventures.

'We heard nothing at all after that and Mr Denniston left society altogether. We looked for him again, then, but had no luck in locating him.' Aunt Adeline's gaze dwelt in the past.

'He probably did not wish to be found. He had no relationship with his own family up in York and he began to drink a lot.' She felt a bit disloyal mentioning these things about her father, but she could also see that Great-Aunt Adeline held a great guilt inside because of not being able to find them.

'Thank you for telling me that. Perhaps he drank because of a broken heart, or perhaps he did not truly have a heart. From our first meetings I always thought that was the more likely.'

'I think that was the conclusion I eventually reached as well. He died eight years ago and he never spoke more than a few words to me about my mother.'

'Then that must have been hard on you, Euphemia, and it's even more of a reason to get to know all Elizabeth's good points. She was fearless and daring and while she was also one who did not like being told what to do, her heart was always in the right place.'

So the similarities had ended there, thought Euphemia, for apart from her brief, foolish moments at the Dashwoods' ball, she had been most circumspect and prudent, her guarded existence necessary for survival.

She wished that Augustus could have come here and seen her among this family, among honourable people, people who were related to her through blood and history. He might have seen her in a different light then, as a woman who was not destitute or doomed to live in her stepmother's awful shadow. Perhaps then she would have had more worth.

She wondered what he was doing right now, back in London. Did the sun shine there, too, finally breaking through the February freeze and giving some hope in the process? Or was he on business up north, chasing something of which he did not wish to speak?

She remembered he had called out a name at least twice when he had lain asleep in the cottage. Alice. Was it this woman he was visiting?

There were so many loose ends. Her hand went up to the outline of his ring on the chain. She had kept it, though she should have sent it back with the pearl earrings, but there was something in the ruby that did give her a power, a spiritualism from India she thought then, the home of the transcendent.

But her aunt did not seem to be quite finished.

'Elizabeth blossomed in the weeks we saw her with your father and if I could hazard a guess I would say she was…a girl who enjoyed the sensual. The pleasures of the flesh are not to be decried, either, Euphemia.'

Further guidance? More counsel that came with many meanings?

Another woman might have been shocked by such confidences, but for Mia it was just a part of a puzzle that clicked into place. Her awful experience at the Dashwoods' ball had blighted her trust in everything and everyone, the sensual night dreams she had had for years becoming unbalanced odd yearnings that she could never quite understand. It had taken Augustus and his determination to show her her true nature, to reconnect her to an inner self that liked the passionate as well. A family trait, apparently. Mia could not imagine another octogenarian in England speaking as Adeline had, but she was so grateful for it.

The exhaustion with which she had arrived here was starting to fade and blossom into a new energy, a belief in herself and a hopefulness. The rumours that were spreading about her in London were barely worth thinking of. She had no wish to go back into society there anyway, preferring life in the country with its space and quiet and beauty.

Stanthorpe Hall, the house of Augustus's grandmother, came to mind and she wished she might have been able to see that estate again. It was smaller than Benningbrook Park, but exquisitely made, and she would never forget her time there.

When she looked around her great-aunt had finished her tea and was dozing in the sunshine and Mia leant back against the cushioned chair and smiled, all the time in the world to simply sit here, at the beck and call of no one.

That night Mia was summoned to the library at Benningbrook and arrived downstairs to find Aunt Adeline, Uncle Terence and Cousin Jennifer sitting in the presence of a tall young man dressed in black.

Before them on the table was a ream of papers.

When they saw her all four stood, Adeline using her black cane with the silver handle to steady herself.

'Euphemia,' she said, gesturing for her to find a seat with them. As soon as she did they all sat down again.

'This is Mr King and he is one of the executors of the estate funds and we have asked him here to make a new provision for you.'

Mia could not quite understand what that meant and the newcomer, sensing her qualms, began to speak.

'Your family would like an account opened in the Bank of England in your name, Miss Denniston. They want the first lump sum deposited there and then the interest you earn added to it every quarter.'

He pushed the papers closer to her so that she might read the figures.

It was a fortune. More money than she could ever in her life have imagined.

'Are you sure?'

She addressed this to the three members of her family and her great-aunt answered for the others.

'It is Elizabeth's portion, Euphemia, and we are all in agreement that any monies owing to her should now come to you.'

'It just seems so very generous and I have only just met you all...'

She could not go on because of the lump that was growing in her throat, but Cousin Jennifer had begun to speak anyway.

'You are our hope for the future, Euphemia. We are all becoming quite ancient and the life blood of the place needs to be carried on as it has been for centuries. Your uncle holds the title now, but as he is childless we fear what will happen next.'

Childless? God, they were hoping for heirs to a place that desperately needed them and she could well understand why. It also explained her great-aunt's comments this morning while having tea in the gardens, the one about finding a suitor locally and settling here.

Old estates carried a weight of duty with them. Augustus had told her that once and now she could see first-hand what he meant. The continuity of a family lineage and the responsibility of giving it strength was left to the last person in line and in this case, at Benningbrook Park, she was the last person.

'You do not have to shoulder this alone, Euphemia.' Uncle Terence was speaking now and his tone was kind. 'We shall all help you and there are many years of transfer ahead so the facts and figures shall not need to be learned in a moment and if you do decide, like Jennifer did, not to marry at all we would support you in that, too.'

Her fingers crept up to the pearls at her neck, her mother's pearls, and the ones that her great-aunt had asked her to wear today. Now she knew why. They were a talisman and a touchstone, a way of linking the generations. She could almost imagine her mother beside her urging her on.

When she reached over for the pen Mr King was offering her, she felt only gratitude as she signed the documents. She had a place now, written in law, and more than enough money to survive. She also had relatives around her who wanted to help her and see her thrive.

What would Augustus make of this? she wondered. How would he perceive her now that she was one of the main beneficiaries of the Benningbrook fortune?

She smoothed out the fabric of her newly made gown where it had creased at the skirt. Three seamstresses had come on the day of her arrival here and this morning packages containing a huge array of clothes, shoes, bags, nightwear and hats had appeared, each new thing more beautiful than the last.

She was a different person. She could sometimes feel the confidence that had been so much part of her mother dribbling back into her.

Tonight she would sit down and write a letter to Augustus. She would swallow her pride and tell him all the things she felt for him, all the dreams she'd had and her hopes for a life together.

If he rebuffed her in his reply, then she still had her place here, but if he didn't... She knew entirely that love was too important to be lost on a misunderstanding and Aunt Adeline had encouraged her to keep the lines of communication open.

All over London the gossip mill had been revving. Roddy Thistlewaite had told everyone almost straight away of the revelations that the new heir to Amerleigh had imparted. There could therefore be no doubt about his intentions.

It was as much as Augustus could do to protect her,

his lineage and fortune paving a way for clemency. And if she by some wondrous chance heard of what was being said, she would either come back to claim his hand or dismiss him altogether.

Bram had been the first to tell him his stocks in the marriage market had crumbled somewhat and that he had heard talk of pity. Pity for his unrequited love now that she had not reappeared, pity for the way he had opened his heart, too, to the most notorious gossip in London.

He did not care. Wherever Euphemia was she would know that she meant something to him, more than something.

But still she had not come.

'Perhaps she is gone?'

Augustus sat opposite Bram and said the words that he did not want to think about, words that made his heart wrench violently in his chest and the fury of dread grow. It had been three days now since she had disappeared.

'I cannot believe that after all the enquiries we have made nothing has turned up yet. Not a single word about her or even a whisper.'

'And the mother? What was her lineage?'

'I have no idea, though Euphemia has a set of pearls from her that look very fine.'

A knock at the door had them both turning.

'There is a Mrs Lucille Denniston waiting in the blue salon, sir. She asks if you might give her a moment.'

Without ado he rose.

Lucille Denniston looked uncertain as he joined her.

'I am very sorry to disturb you, Mr Rushworth, but I did not know that you intended to marry my daughter and if I had I should certainly not have acted in the way I did. I was only trying to protect her, you see, and for her not to have come back after you have been so kind...'

He did not let her finish.

'Do you know where Euphemia's mother was from, Mrs Denniston?'

'I do.' She remained silent and Augustus realised she was waiting for some payment for her service.

He pulled out some coins from his purse and handed them over and she continued on.

'She was Miss Elizabeth—I don't know her family name—from Sevenoaks, I think Lionel had said, for he was helping her uncle catalogue some library when he met her. He used to do that sort of work once upon a time. He was an academic, you understand, until we began to fall on hard times and he started to drink a lot.'

'How old was your husband when they were married?'

'Twenty-six. She was eighteen and Lionel implied that she was badly spoilt and fell into a depression almost as soon as she was pregnant with Euphemia. It was a doomed marriage.'

Things were beginning to come together. Euphemia had told him her mother had only been married to her father for a year and had passed away when she was born. The clues were mounting up. He would drive down to Sevenoaks in Kent this afternoon to see if there was any sign of the family there for surely someone must have known a young Miss Elizabeth even if they were only moderately wealthy.

After Mrs Denniston had left he told Bram all she had said and he was full of fury at the woman for expecting payment for information that might help her stepdaughter.

'To think that Euphemia Denniston was stuck with her for all those years. It explains why she sometimes looked so sad.'

'Her father was as bad, for he drank away any money to which they could once lay claim.'

'You will go down to Sevenoaks, August?'

'I will. I can no longer just sit here waiting, Bram. I have to find her.'

'What if she does not wish to be found?'

'If she tells me that to my face and means it, then I will return straight back to London. It's been four days since she disappeared and anything would be an improvement to finding out that she is…dead.'

He breathed out as he said this. The whole damn thing was his fault. Why had he not professed his love for her in the cottage on his grandmother's estate? Why had he taken her home to the awful house on Bolton Street and left her there to be vilified by her stepmother and given the cut direct by all the rest of society?

He had protected her almost as little as Lucille Denniston had, his mind only on getting the licence and having the right ring. If he really had lost her…

'When Christina was taken by her uncle back to Leicester, I thought she was gone from me, too. But she wasn't. Misunderstandings can be resolved, August.'

'At least you knew who had taken her, Bram. Perhaps the carriage that was seen on the street outside my house held people who would want to hurt Euphemia. She is just so damn beautiful—' He stopped because he knew if he went on he never would be able to stop.

He needed to regain his balance and his sense. He needed to find her and at least now he had a place to start. Sevenoaks. He could get there by nightfall.

'If Tony returns with other information, will you promise to get someone to bring it down to me, Bram? I will let my men know to contact you.'

'Of course.'

The Chequers Coaching Inn on the High Street had a room and stables. Leaving his men to deal with the horses, he entered the tavern, meaning to make an immediate start.

The innkeeper was a round and ruddy man who looked like someone who enjoyed talking. After the introductions, Augustus put forward his question.

'Miss Elizabeth?' He looked perplexed. 'There are of course a number of girls by that name...'

'No, the Miss Elizabeth I am after is long dead, but it is the family I am seeking. She would have lived here near on thirty years ago.'

'I will ask around for you, sir, but I wouldn't hold out much luck. Know all the families in this area, I do, and I can't think of anyone that would fit your description.'

The dead end made Augustus uneasy, but it was late and so he ordered supper and decided to eat it downstairs just in case there were others who might remember her.

He asked the barmaid and the man who was carrying a large keg of wine through the room. He asked the cook, too, when she came out to see how he liked his meal and he asked the couple on the table next to him, elderly local folk who might have had such a memory.

But no one could help him.

It was after eleven when he decided to go to his room and it had begun to snow again. Did this blasted weather never stop? he thought. He was just finishing his third beer of the night when he heard the sound of a carriage coming in late. The next moment Bram appeared with Tony by his side.

'The family live just outside Sevenoaks, August, in a place called Benningbrook Park. It is the estate of Lord Aldridge, the Fifth Earl of Benningbrook. It's a grand old home on a thousand acres.'

August turned to the innkeeper who had come over to see who the new arrivals were. 'Where is Benningbrook Park?'

'Go along the High Street here and turn left at the road that next runs across it. You will find the Park about five miles down. I have never been there myself, but the owners are good people who are rarely seen in town. They keep to themselves, mind, so they might not be that happy to see you.'

Augustus was astonished at what the man was saying. Could these be Euphemia's people, her family? Had Euphemia's mother been related to an earl? Lucille Denniston had spoken of her husband being asked to catalogue a library. That fitted.

Please God, he found himself praying. *Please make Euphemia be there. Let the family that was still living have found her on the street outside his place on the night she disappeared.*

Perhaps they had been searching for her, too, and it was only in his company in society that she had begun to be truly visible again. Everyone at the Barretts' ball had been speaking of her loveliness in the golden gown. Could such gossip have reached Sevenoaks and led them to her?

If it had not been so late and snowing he would have saddled a horse and ridden out to the place this minute, but it was almost twelve o'clock and there would be nothing to do about it tonight.

Instead, he ordered two more rooms for Bram and Tony and after toasting their success with a brandy each he took himself up to his room where he stood at the window and looked into the darkness.

'Are you here, Euphemia? Are you close?'

His fingers clasped the bracelet Alice had given him, his fingers running across the markings. She had been a child of the Indian way and had always believed in signs.

When he looked out of the window again a moment later, the snow had stopped and a full moon had broken through the gap in the clouds, sending a shimmering light across the landscape. Like a pathway. Suddenly he found himself praying for the first time in years, praying to a God he once thought had deserted him, but who had brought Euphemia into his life.

One life gone and another one gained. Love lost and then found. The circle of it gave him comfort and peace and in the morning as soon as the sun was up he would go to Benningbrook Park.

Euphemia awoke to a day that was totally white, though the sky was blue and the sun was shining.

She'd dreamt of Augustus again, a vivid joyful dream, the same dream she had had every night since the cottage. He was telling her he loved her and that he wanted to marry her and that everything else had been a mistake. She decided that today she would have the message she'd written delivered to his town house. If he did not come then, she would know that it was over.

An hour later there was a knock on her door and her Cousin Jennifer scurried in.

'There is someone from London here to see you, Mia. It is Mr Rushworth. He does not appear to be a haughty man at all, certainly he is unlike anything I had imagined…'

'He is here?' Euphemia broke across her cousin's words. It was as if the night-time dreams and the daytime reality had collided, crashing against each other in a perfect storm. She felt the breath leave her throat at the same time as her blood rushed to her face and she sat down. Abruptly.

'Should we tell him to leave? We can do that if you would rather?'

'No. I need to see him. Is Aunt Adeline with him?'

'She is and she looks like the cat who got the cream. Is there something I don't know, something you haven't told me? Aunt Adeline is smiling.'

'I know you are aware that we have been intimate. What you do not know is that I love him, with all of my heart.'

'And he loves you back?'

'That is what I am about to find out.'

'Well, why would he come here otherwise and at this hour of the morning? If he did not think so highly of you, wouldn't he simply have had a message delivered or not come at all?'

Hope flared, as did a desperate desire for all she had dreamed of. Crossing to the mirror, she looked at herself and decided that the dark blue gown she had on today suited her and with her hair pulled casually back into a knot she also looked…herself. She did not wish to meet him as a stranger, as the heir to the Benningbrook fortune, as the grand-niece of an earl.

Too much had come between them for veils and mirrors. She dug down into her bodice and extracted her golden chain, placing his ruby ring in full view. A powerful ring of energy and passion. Today she was glad of it.

Halfway down the stairs she stopped and took in three deep breaths. Counting in, holding, breathing out. She had not done this at all at Benningbrook Park and that realisation surprised her. But in the next few moments she would know the shape her life might take and it was terrifying.

A short walk down a hall and then she was at the door to the library. It was open and she could hear his voice again, so dear, so familiar. Tears sprang to her eyes.

It was Adeline who saw her first, her great-aunt's face softened by a smile, and as she stood he turned, towards her, the sun from the windows catching his hair and his eyes.

'Euphemia.' He strode forward and caught her to him. She felt his hands on her checking that she was real and here and unharmed.

'Euphemia?' His voice held delight and relief, the undertone of question left for now while he savoured her. 'I have been looking everywhere for you. They said a carriage picked you up and I had no idea where to search…'

He stopped and swallowed and she suddenly found herself crying, the tears falling properly now, wetting the fabric in his sleeves.

She looked like a daughter of this household now, no patched-up, second-hand gown upon her, but one of a dark blue velvet, fitted properly and of the very best quality. She also wore his ring there at her breast, a quiet statement that he had not been forgotten and so perhaps...

The old aunt was speaking now, her voice soft and her eyes sparkling.

'I think we should leave Euphemia and Mr Rushworth for a few moments, Jennifer, for they will have much to say to one another.' The woman behind nodded in agreement.

Then they were gone and the door was shut, leaving them alone here in the library, the silence broken only by the sounds of their breathing.

'Why on earth did you run away?' He had to ask this of her, though he held her to him as she answered as if she might disappear again if he let her go.

'You said you did not expect what had happened between us and that you were sorry. It did not seem like the words or actions of a man who wanted to take things further and I was too raw and too in love to want to stay around and hear that.'

'In love? With me?'

'Of course. Did you not know that, August?'

'I hoped for it, but I was fixed on making everything right again after our night together. I wanted things to be perfect for you. I wanted you to stay with me for ever.'

'I came to see you to return the pearl earrings. Your butler said you had gone from London and that you would not be back for a few days. I thought perhaps you had gone to see the woman who you called out for in the night when you were dreaming.'

'What woman?'

'Alice. Her name was Alice.'

'No, goodness, no...' He clutched her tighter. 'Alice was my daughter. She was seven and I lost her in India to the cholera. I loved her more than life itself.' He smiled. 'I loved her as I love you, Euphemia, without reservation, without question and without thinking.'

Her beautiful blue eyes watched him, bathed in tears, and one finger came up to blot them away.

'Will you marry me, Mia? Will you be my wife? Please.'

This scene was nothing like he had imagined it might be, no music, no flowers, no ring. He had not even got down on one knee.

But he didn't want to let her go even for a second and he no longer needed all the supports he had thought he did. Love was simple and easy and plain, it was much stronger than pretence and illusion when it held no secrets.

She was his and he was hers.

'Yes, of course I will marry you, August, but there are things I have not told you about me...'

'Nothing could make a difference. I love you just as you are.'

He took the golden chain off her neck by undoing the clasp and then he held the ruby ring out to her.

'I know it is yours already, but you have my heart,

Euphemia, and my soul and my body. Will you take my name, too?'

'I will.'

Her smile was broad now and he thought of that first time when he had seen her at the dock by the Frost Fair. She had knocked him off balance and he had never recovered. Love at first sight was something he had not believed in until now, yet here he was, a man who was nothing if she was not in his life.

He dug into his pocket and brought out the licence he had procured the second day after he had lost her.

'I want to be married as soon as we can.'

'Today. There is a chapel here at Benningbrook Park and a minister can be found.'

'You do not wish for bridesmaids or a wedding dress?'

'No, you are all that I want, August, a man who understands me and makes me truly happy. My Great-Aunt Adeline says that the women in our family have a passionate nature and you showed me that was true.'

He groaned, hearing in the sound an echo of lust.

Three hours later and standing in a dress the colour of light peach she and August were married in the small but beautiful Benningbrook Park chapel, to the sound of music, among the smell of flowers and standing within the love of her family circle. Bramwell Baker-Hall and Tony Ferris were there, too, fetched from the tavern as his witnesses and both with wide smiles on their faces. It was fitting that they were present as he had known them since he was a boy and they had been the ones to point Augustus in the right direction to find her.

Great-Aunt Adeline was the matron of honour and both Cousin Jennifer and Great-Uncle Terence signed the register as well. Euphemia had a bouquet of snow-drops and winter jasmine, English primrose and hel-lebores, all from the Park gardens and in a variety of shades. August had a single white English primrose threaded through the buttonhole of his jacket and he had tied his hair back in a thick plaited leather band.

He looked beautiful and strong and happy and after the vows were said and the speeches were finished they repaired to a wing of the house she had not seen before with Great-Aunt Adeline and Cousin Jennifer.

'This was the part of Benningbrook Park that your mother loved best, my dear. We will have a dinner sent over and the place has been readied for you. I hope it is to your satisfaction.'

Flowers were everywhere, many of the same variet-ies that were in her bouquet, but there were also other blooms that she had no names for.

In the middle of the second room was a large bed made up for a winter night though a fire also burned in the grate to one side.

'It is beautiful and my wedding was, too.'

After bidding them goodnight, Mia watched them go for they both meant the world to her. But the one who was her everything stood before her, his eyes gentle and kind.

'Your family is lovely and you suit them.'

She laughed. 'When they brought me down here I was heartbroken, but now I have everything I want and that everything is you.'

Mia reached for the line of his lips and traced across it lightly with her finger. Then she dropped her touch to his collar and his chest, her fingers lingering over the buttons that held his waistcoat closed.

'May I undress you?' She waited till he nodded.

A few moments later he was naked, his body glowing in the light of what was left of the day and of the fire.

He did not look at her as she walked around him, but stood there still and unmoving.

'I can see that you want me, August.'

He smiled. 'The body of a man is not made for subtlety.'

'But it is made for loving.'

When she smiled his reserve broke. He lifted her to him and she felt her shoes fall, one by one, to the floor.

'My turn, sweetheart.'

When he laid her on the bed he watched her, his whole face wreathed in desire. Then he bent and saw that her gown, the ties and buttons were dispensed with, as was her petticoat.

Now all she wore was her white stockings with their pink-flowered garters and in her hair the buds of winter jasmine still lingered.

She was the most beautiful woman he could have imagined, her legs long and slender, her skin pale, her dimples dancing in her cheeks.

He lay down and took her gently and without haste.

He took her like a man who couldn't believe his luck that he had not found her broken.

He felt his restraint and his control even as he entered her, with care and with discipline—the wetness inside was a welcome discovery for it told him how much she wanted him as well.

They did not speak but rather felt, each second and minute, each touch, each quiet reminder of the other, until the heat took them into urgency and all restraint was gone.

Afterwards he lay with her tucked in beside him, pulling the counterpane up over her nakedness, watching the dancing shadows that the fire made.

'I love you.' He said the words slowly as if every one of them was important.

'I love you, too.' Her fingers brushed the scars on his arm, the ones she had never asked about but now did.

'What happened?'

'I was just eighteen and my brother attacked me.'

'Why?'

'He was a man who had no morality and I had told him so. He'd hurt a friend's sister badly and I said if he ever did anything like that again I would kill him. At the time I meant it. He was a bully without honour or limitations.'

'So he tried to kill you?'

'My father came home and saw us fighting and he told my brother that I would never understand the power and passion of the Rushworths and that I was not worth the trouble of an argument. He said that I was my mother's child and that he doubted he had anything at all to do with my conception. Jeremy, my brother, called me a bastard and other names that were much worse. He said he could hurt anyone he wanted and would, and that no one, especially me, could stop him. I think by then he was drunk and when he grabbed a sword and dragged it down across my arm more than once all I saw was blood. I knew then that he was trying to kill me and in answer I picked up another sword and tried to beat him back. When he lunged forward at me the tip of my weapon ran through the top of his leg and my father attacked me with almost as much malice.'

'Who stopped it, then? Two against one was hardly fair.'

'My grandfather. He grabbed me by the scruff of my neck and pulled me out of there and sent me to India.'

Euphemia sat and listened, every word he said more terrible than the last. But secrets scarred one inside and out and it was time for the truth to come from her, too.

'It was your brother Jeremy who abused me at the Dashwoods' ball.'

'My love, no...'

'Then he sent one of his men to waylay me the next day outside our house. I could see your brother sitting in the carriage, watching me but as I ran I tripped, and screamed and screamed until others came. When they did he left, his man following, and I knew then just how much of a danger he was to me. It was a scandal and I

didn't go back into society for years. I never told any-
body who it was, either.'

'So he got away with it? Damn him. If he had not
died when he did in some duel with an angry husband,
he would have been hanged sooner or later. I certainly
did not mourn his passing.'

'That makes two of us,' she answered back and snug-
gled in closer.

'So many secrets between us, Euphemia. So many
things we could not say to each other.'

'For fear.'

'And for love.'

She knew he meant Alice and pointed to the bracelet he had taken off and laid on the table by the bed.

'What does it mean?' She wanted to know.

'*"Our body is love. We are eternal."* Alice gave me
the bracelet a month or so before she died and I chose
the engraving. When I lost you the words kept me sane
because no matter what happened I knew I would find
you again and that we would be together, in life or in
death.'

'I want us to live at your grandmother's estate, August. I want to have lots of children and to live there.'

'What of here? What of Benningbrook Park and the
family you have just found again after so long?'

'We need our space and we will visit here often, but
I want a new beginning, away from my mother and
father and Lucille and the past. I want to see the garden of Stanthorpe Hall in the springtime and pick the
roses in summer, great enormous bunches of them to

fill the house. And the cottage shall be only our place, our sanctuary.'

'A home for us both. A place to stop and put down roots?'

'Exactly.'

Epilogue

Stanthorpe Hall—Christmas, 1816

Everyone was there, filling the house with laughter and joy, and Stanthorpe Hall rang with the voices of excited children waiting for the next treat. Joining in with the little Balcombes, Baker-Hills and Forsythes was the sound of a younger child, crying amid the chaos.

Augustus went to pick Alistair up, his little son calming the minute he did so.

'Do you think you're missing out?' he said as he carried him in to his wife. 'Did you think we had forgotten you?'

Anna Balcombe smiled. 'He's growing before my very eyes, I swear he is, and he is the spitting image of you, August.'

'I want a girl next then, Euphemia, with blonde hair and dimples,' he joked as she gently rocked Alistair back to sleep. 'Aunt Adeline looks like she might, too.'

Across the room her great-aunt was sitting very still

as the three-year-old Forsythe daughter was doing her hair, or what was left of it. The white strands shone pale beneath the candlelight. Cousin Jennifer was watching them.

Over in another corner, the Earl of Aldridge was discussing politics with Bram and Christina and Tony Ferris, the corner dissolving into laughter at something Terence said.

'Your great-uncle has a keen sense of humour.'

'Something that is quite recent, according to Cousin Jennifer. She said that after our marriage he has been more energetic and interested in life as each day passes. He has even taken up gardening.'

When she smiled, Augustus could only think of how lucky he was and of how he had come full circle in life since meeting Euphemia.

He had felt lost and now he was found. He had been broken in India and Euphemia had healed him. Just as he had healed her, he thought next, the sensuality she brought to their bed a hidden treasure.

She wanted more children, too, and quickly, and he was more than obliging in her request.

Tonight, after this celebration, they would go to their room and make love with the moonlight spilling in upon them. The fire would play upon her stomach, ripe from the child she had told him about last evening that grew even now inside her. A Christmas present, she had said, but it was much more than that.

It was the joy of love and the ease of it. It was in the laughter and the whispered confidences. It was in family and place and home. And in the flowers she insisted upon picking at every given season and which she brought inside in bunches.

His grandmother would have loved her, August thought, and even his grandfather was coming over to Stanthorpe Hall more often now, something he had not wanted at first, but Euphemia had been determined to make him welcome. She had invited her stepsister Susan over to see them, too, though as yet she had not taken up the offer.

'Family is family,' she said, 'and Alice, from her place in Heaven, will rejoice to see us all together. No one we love is to be lost, August, ever again.'

'Lost like we were, you mean?'

She smiled and pulled him down into her and he knew that was exactly what she meant.

* * * * *